# GHOST

F
SLA
PB

Slade, Arthur

Ghost hotel
18-Capilano

ARTHUR SLADE'S CANADIAN CHILLS #2

# GHOST HOTEL

ARTHUR SLADE

COTEAU BOOKS

Edited by Robert Currie.
Book and cover design by Duncan Campbell.
Cover image montage by Duncan Campbell. Source photos by Zach Hauser, and Photonica.

Printed and bound in Canada at Gauvin Press.


Library and Archives Canada Cataloguing in Publication

Slade, Arthur G. (Arthur Gregory)
Ghost hotel / Arthur Slade.

(Arthur Slade's Canadian chills ; #2)
ISBN 1-55050-306-5

I. Title. II. Series.

PS8587.L343G46 2004    jC813'.54    C2004-904995-X


1  2  3  4  5  6  7  8  9  10

401-2206 Dewdney Ave.
Regina, Saskatchewan
Canada    S4R 1H3

*Available in the US and Canada from:*
Fitzhenry & Whiteside
195 Allstate Parkway
Markham, Ontario
Canada    L3R 4T8

The publisher gratefully acknowledges the financial assistance of the Saskatchewan Arts Board, t
Canada Council for the Arts, the Government of Canada through the Book Publishing Indust
Development Program (BPIDP), and the City of Regina Arts Commission, for its publishing program.

*This book is dedicated to
the affable and amicable residents
of Nutana neighbourhood.*

CHAPTER ONE

# OUT OF NOWHERE

y only goal was to kill the pesky yellow bird.

It came at me, arcing through the air as I jumped off the gym floor, and pulled back my racquet for the perfect smash. At that very same moment, I sensed that someone on the stage was staring at me. I swung heroically but missed; the birdie dropped to the floor and bounced. I landed in a jumbled pile of arms and legs, my knees thudding into the floor.

"Wart! What are you doing?" Cindy muttered. Cindy is my best friend and my badminton partner. She's red-haired, thin, spunky, and suffers from an acute case of impatientitis. "We're trying to win here. We've got the twins on the ropes. Concentrate!"

Amber and Anna, the frizzy-haired Pennock twins,

1

watched us like raptors from across the net. They were the best Grade Seven players in Victoria School. We wanted to claim that title and so had challenged them to an after-school grudge match.

"Someone was staring at me," I said, looking at the empty stage. "My ESP senses detected it."

"You don't have ESP!"

"Well, my detective senses, then." We were the only four people in the gym. I looked back at the stage. Still empty. "Someone's watching us right now."

"*I'm* staring at you," Cindy said. "I'm staring and hoping you'll stand up and get one more point. That's all we need, Wart."

I slowly got to my feet. My real name is Walter Biggar Bronson, though my friends call me Wart. Not that I have any warts (though I once had one on my right thumb), but because I'm a worrywart. Cute, eh? I brushed off my knees, grabbed my racquet, and glanced quickly back at the stage. The curtain was moving.

"Wait a second!" I took a step off the court. "I want to check –"

Cindy grabbed my shoulder. "No, Wart. Not another step. You're always wandering off at the wrong moment. Finish the game."

I breathed in, getting ready to launch into a brilliant argument. I opened my mouth.

"They're probably gone, anyway," Cindy announced, before I could say anything. "If they were there at all."

I shrugged, grabbed the birdie and served, but Amber smashed it right back at me. The twins took their turn, tying the game at fourteen points. Now, because of my goof-up, we'd have to play to three points. Whoever got there first would win. I readied myself, but I couldn't concentrate. Before I knew it we were tied at two points each. Cindy served. I glanced at the stage. I was sure I saw someone there – just a vague shape.

"Wart!" she yelled.

The bird was coming towards me but I was frozen, not sure what to do. Cindy leapt like a leopard, rolled like a ninja, then popped up and smashed the bird down, winning the game.

"Yes!" she said.

I patted her back, but I was still...well...worried about what I thought I'd seen. When we shook hands with the Pennock twins, mine was cold and clammy.

"Well, we pulled it off," Cindy said on the way out of the gym.

"You pulled it off. I'm sorry, I was so sure there was someone else in the gym. I felt beady eyes watching me."

"How did you know they were beady?"

"In my business they're always beady." The business I was talking about was the Walter Biggar Bronson Ghost

Detective and Time Travel Agency. I was the Chief Executive Officer, of course, and Cindy was my sidekick. We had been open for a year and had yet to crack our first case. Or, actually, to even be offered one.

"Well, I'm going to towel off," Cindy said. "And tease the twins. I'll catch up with you in a few minutes."

I changed, went to my locker, and undid the lock, my hands still feeling clammy. I was cooling down quickly, partly because Victoria School is a giant brick building, designed to be drafty (it was built in 1909 and named after an old British queen who'd probably never heard of Saskatoon). I swear some of the teachers have been here since the school opened.

I felt a tap on my shoulder. "What do you want, Cindy?"

She didn't say anything.

"What do you want?" I repeated.

She tapped again. My shoulder felt as though it were freezing, ice creeping into my veins. A chill ran slowly down my spine, and the hair on the back of my neck began to rise.

"Cindy?" I whispered. "It is you, right?"

I slowly turned. There was no one there – only an empty hallway, with flickering lights. I blinked and was surprised to see that a boy now stood right in front of me.

He had seemingly appeared out of nowhere. Or else

I'd somehow missed seeing him. He had a lost and sad look on his face, as though he'd witnessed some unimaginably awful thing. He was dressed in a nerdy grey suit-and-tie outfit and a bowler hat that made him look like a mini-version of Charlie Chaplin. The lights flickered, so that he disappeared for a second and appeared again.

I blinked. Something had to be wrong with my vision.

Immediately my detective mind kicked into gear. I noted that his clothing was an out-of-date style, possibly from the fifties or earlier. His feet were bare, and he seemed to be floating a few centimetres above the floor. It had to be an optical illusion. I stared at his feet. They were perfectly clean. Somewhere in my encyclopedic mind I remembered one simple but chilling fact: people are often buried without their shoes.

Which meant that he had been buried.

Which meant that he was dead.

My hands began to shake. My watch glowed and made an *eep* sound. It has a band of electro-ectoplasm around it that lights up whenever a supernatural presence comes near. At least that's what my dad told me it would do. I had never seen it glow before. It also has a werewolf alarm, but nothing for vampires. They rarely travel this far north, because they don't like the cold. It makes the blood thin.

Anyway, the glowing on my watch made another chill run over my spine and confirmed my suspicions. I was standing eye to eye with a ghost.

CHAPTER TWO

# GOING UP

The boy stared at me with huge grey eyes, on the edge of crying. His mouth moved silently.

"Uh, hello," I said.

He lifted a tiny pale hand and pointed behind him. The hall was empty.

"Is there something you want me to see?" I asked.

He nodded, slowly turned, and walked away. I grabbed my jacket, gloves, and earmuffs, and followed.

We passed Cindy just as she was putting her gym clothes in her hall locker. She looked up. I made our hand signal for ghost, a closed fist raised in the air with my pinky pointing skyward.

"What?" she yelled. "There's a gremlin in the school? What kind?"

I quickly put my index finger to my lip to signify silence, something she wasn't good at. I pointed at the boy, then at my glowing watch. She squinted and her eyes widened to the size of baseballs.

"There's a boy there!" she exclaimed. "I didn't see him at first. Who is he?"

"He's a ghost," I whispered. "He must've been the one watching us from the stage."

She slammed her locker door shut and joined me, pulling on her coat. "He doesn't look like a ghost," she said. "More like he was in an olden-days movie or something. Are you sure he's not just lost and wandering around?"

"He has no shoes," I pointed out. "He's obviously a ghost."

"Well, maybe he forgot them. His feet must be freezing. You know how kids are today."

The boy was getting farther ahead of us, so we sped up, but couldn't get any closer. Shimmering in and out of focus, he walked right through the front doors without opening them.

"Did you see that?" I asked.

"Holy mackerel! He *is* a ghost!" she exclaimed. "This is our first real case!" By the way, Cindy swears fish names all the time. Her dad is a guide; he spends the summers up north, guiding American fisherpeople through the bush, so that they can catch fish and release them. "It's not even the witching hour."

It was gently snowing outside, the perfect November evening. The glimmering boy led us down the Broadway Bridge. My eyes were drawn to the Bessborough Hotel, lit up like an art display. Lights on both sides of the South Saskatchewan river glittered. Well, except for the lights along the bridge that dimmed as the ghost drew closer, and brightened after he passed. He obviously had a powerful energy field around him. Ghosts will turn out batteries in flashlights or make your cellphone buzz, but few have enough energy to affect street lights.

"Jumping brook trout!" Cindy said. "He's like a walking ectoplasmic factory."

Ectoplasm, by the way, is that slimy stuff that oozes from ghosts, allowing them to materialize in our world. It smells like burnt chocolate and looks a lot like runny snot. Green runny snot. You know the kind you get when you've had a cold for three days straight and you blow your nose and examine your hankie. That's exactly what ectoplasm looks like.

The boy went down the stone steps to Spadina and followed the sidewalk. Even the street lights dimmed. He cut across the road.

A car was speeding straight for him.

"Watch out!" I yelled.

The car kept going and the ghost walked on, paying no attention to the vehicle. The headlights went black as the car drove through the boy. The driver hit the brakes and screeched to a stop. He flicked his headlights several times, and they slowly glowed yellow, then returned to their original brightness. He probably hadn't even seen the ghost. He must've stepped lightly on the gas because he disappeared down Spadina as if he were driving a pedal car.

The boy was across the street already, walking along without a backward glance. Cindy and I looked both ways before crossing. The ghost was heading for the Delta Bessborough, the castle in the centre of our city. Well, a hotel really, but it looks like a castle with tall walls, spires, a copper-clad roof, and leering gargoyles and grotesques on every corner. No matter which side of the moatlike river you're on, your eyes are drawn to the Bess.

The boy stopped in front of the big glass doors of the hotel. He waited, tapping his foot, eyes level with the golden door handles.

We watched.

"Why is he waiting?" I asked. "He could walk right through."

"Maybe it's a ritual or something," Cindy suggested.

The doorman, an old guy dressed in a brown suit,

opened the door and stood looking around. He was Einstein's twin – hair sticking out every which way from under his cap. Perhaps he watched a scary movie every day before work. The boy walked into the hotel. The doorman scratched his head and closed the door.

We ran up, and the doorman opened the door. "Good evening, young sir, young miss, welcome to the Delta Bessborough. I guess it was you I opened the door for just a few seconds ago." He still looked puzzled. "I must have known you were coming."

"Thank you," I said. I would have liked to quiz him about perhaps "sensing" a presence, but there wasn't time. We had to catch up to the ghost.

In front of us, down a set of stairs, was the massive check-in desk, surrounded on either side by luxurious leather couches. The smell of sizzling steak drifted into the room from the Samurai Restaurant. Above us, there was an opening in the ceiling so you could see the mezzanine. But where was our ghost? I looked left towards the entrance to the Samurai. All I saw were salivating hotel guests. I glanced to the right and caught a glimpse of him climbing the stairs to the mezzanine. We quickly followed, and just as we reached the top of the staircase, I spotted him in front of the elevators.

Cindy tried to step past me, but I grabbed her arm and whispered, "Hold up. I don't want to be on the same elevator as a ghost with that much ectopower. Electronics could fail and make the elevator crash."

The doors opened, he floated in, and they closed.

"But he's getting away," Cindy said. Her eyebrows narrowed; she was focused.

"Just wait. I know what I'm doing. At least I think I do."

We walked up and watched the elevator lights. They stopped on the fifth floor.

"He's getting off on the fifth," Cindy said. "Let's go."

The fourth floor and the sixth lit up at the same time. The lights made a *zap* noise and conked out.

"What does that mean?" I asked.

"It means take the other elevator."

We got on the other elevator. Out of habit, I checked my watch: 7:43 p.m. A good detective always knows what time it is. That way you never miss a coffee break.

Cindy punched the buttons. "Fifth floor," she hit it. "No, it was the fourth."

"No, dummy, it was the sixth floor," I said, scowling at her. I reached out, and we hit the buttons for the fourth and sixth floors at the same time.

"Oh, great, Wart," Cindy said. "Now who knows who was right?"

The elevator hummed up to the fifth floor and stopped, but the doors didn't budge. We had a moment to look at each other. Cindy opened her mouth to say something, but then the elevator plummeted to the fourth floor. My stomach, along with all its gurgling contents, rose quickly. The elevator thudded to a stop so suddenly that I nearly collapsed.

"That was fun," Cindy said, sarcastically. She hit the Door Open button. "We're stuck! Suffering sturgeon! We're really stuck! We're gonna die here! They'll find our bones and our clothes. I'll be late with my math homework."

"At least you'll finally have a good excuse."

I tried to pull the doors open, but they refused to move. Cindy joined in. "Well," I said, after half a minute of straining, "I've thought hard about our situation and looked at it from every possible angle. We don't want to make a wrong move. So this is my conclusion: we'll have to press the Emergency button."

"Go ahead. I've always wanted to see what would happen."

"What will happen," I said, the authority of a CEO creeping into my voice, "is a bell will ring at the front desk, and within a few minutes we will be rescued by friendly hotel employees. Maybe we'll get a free sundae or an *I Love the Bess* T-shirt."

I reached out and pressed the red button. It made a click sound, but nothing else happened. I pressed it again, so hard my finger cracked.

The elevator jerked into life, gears grinding. It shot up, up to the sixth floor, so quickly we were thrown to our knees. I felt dizzy and a little disoriented. Just as we pulled ourselves to our feet the elevator dropped several floors in two seconds and shuddered to a complete stop on the mezzanine floor.

"Apparently the Emergency button creates an emergency," Cindy said.

The doors opened, and a man in a grey suit strode into the elevator. He tipped his fedora hat. "Evening, kiddos," he said.

# CHAPTER THREE

# TORTLING

"Uh, good evening," I answered as we hesitantly stepped out. The doors closed behind us.

We weren't on the mezzanine, but rather in what looked like the lobby. It was busy; several men in old-style suits were in line to check in, brown suitcases sitting at their feet like patient dogs. The ladies were seated on leather couches and plush chairs, their dresses fancy, their hair tied up in buns. An electric chandelier hung from the ceiling.

"What floor is this?" Cindy asked.

I shrugged. "Maybe it's a costume ball. Everyone is dressed up in olden-days clothes. Weird, eh?"

The clerk put a message in a pneumatic tube and it was sucked upwards.

"That's weird. They don't have pneumatic tubes in the Bess any more," I said.

"Holy halibut!" Cindy exclaimed. She slugged my shoulder. "You made us go back into the past."

"Not on purpose!" I said, looking around at all the signs that we were in another era. Even the lobby phone was a big wooden box with a black receiver. It really was the past. I hoped we wouldn't be trapped here. "Don't worry...uh...we're smart enough that we'll find our way back. We might as well enjoy ourselves while we're here. In fact, I need to sit down."

We found two chairs in an alcove and sat. The hotel patrons were gabbing away, the chandelier burning bright above them. The floor looked familiar. "This *is* the mezzanine," I said. "Everything is exactly the same as the mezzanine in the future. Except that!" I motioned to my left at the floor.

"Except what?"

"There's no floor like that in the Bess today. In fact, there's nothing at all."

She looked around. "You're right. They cut it all away so you're able to look down into the lobby."

"You *will* be able to," I corrected. "In the future."

"Oh yeah. So in the old days they checked in on the mezzanine. Wow, people must have been stronger back then."

"Why?"

"To carry all their luggage upstairs."

I sometimes wonder if Cindy's brain cells have their own logic.

A hotel maid in a black-and-white dress strolled quickly by. She had a straw broom clutched in her hand. I tried to look nonchalant, hoping not to attract any attention. A guy in a grey suit walked past, not even bothering to glance in our direction.

"No one's staring at us," I said.

"Do you expect them to? Is my hair that bad?" She touched the top of her head. "Yours is."

"No." I felt my rooster tail, in the same place as always. "I mean, no one notices we're dressed differently. We're in jeans and you – you have your *Spiffy Girls* sweatshirt on. I told you to always be ready for anything, including time travel. What kind of sidekick are you?"

"Sidekick!" She elbowed me right below the kidney. "Flipping fish sticks! I'm not a sidekick. We're partners! Equals! A sidekick implies a...a seniority in our relationship. It's completely –" She stopped as another maid walked by, also carrying a broom. There had to be quite a mess somewhere. She looked similar to the first one; maybe she was a sister.

"See," I said. "We really aren't drawing any attention. Except for your fishy curses, of course."

"They're exclamations! And we'll talk about the side-kick situation when we're back in the office. Right now I'll focus on our task." Cindy glanced around. "Well, it's obvious that we're in the thirties: 1936, to be exact."

"How can you tell?" I asked. Maybe she deserved a promotion from sidekick. She seemed to be thinking fast, a good sign for a detective. "Is it the style of clothes? The artwork on the walls? Carbon-14 dating?"

"No, I looked at the calendar." Cindy pointed at the check-in desk.

"February 13th, 1936. Wow! We have gone back. My mom and dad weren't even born. People hadn't even landed on the moon."

"Or invented Game Boys," Cindy added.

A businessman walked by. He tipped his fedora to us.

"Those hats sure were popular," Cindy whispered. "A whole generation of hat hair."

A bellboy lugged suitcases past us as though they were crammed full of bricks. His hair was greasy.

"Wart, let's get a move on," Cindy said. "There's got to be a way out of here."

"Not until we find the little boy," I said, patiently – or as though I was talking to a patient. "We must approach this situation cautiously and carefully. We must be logical and precise. We must be the ultimate detectives."

"Okay, okay," she said, "you're boring me with details. I just don't want to be stuck here. Everyone's skin is too pale. And the men have motor oil in their hair."

"It's Brylcreem, Cindy," I corrected. I scanned the lobby, my detective-trained eyes looking for the details within the details. "He's got to be here. There aren't too many kids. Mostly businessmen and women."

"How are we going to find him? Just yell his name?"

"If we knew it, that would help."

"Maybe we should pretend we're looking for our room. C'mon."

She grabbed my hand and pulled me towards the front desk. "We haven't made a plan," I said. "You have to make a plan and follow it to the letter. And we need two backup plans."

"Stop babbling like a bubble-headed brook trout, Wart!" she said. "We'll improvise."

She yanked my arm, and I stumbled after her. My foot got caught on the carpet, and I headed for the floor. Cindy tried to hold me up, but the next thing you know, we banged into the front desk and fell to our knees.

The perturbed night clerk peered down at us. He had small, round glasses that magnified his eyes to double their size. A line of dead spiders rested on his upper lip. I blinked. No, not spiders, it was a thin moustache. "How may I be of service?" he asked haughtily. He was wearing a white shirt and suspenders.

We both stood up, using the desk as support. "Uh," Cindy said. "We, uh..."

"Nice improv," I whispered. "We're looking for our friend," I said.

"Yeah," Cindy chimed in. "His parents are here with him. They told us to go see them in their room."

"And what would your friend's surname be?"

"Sure name?" Cindy answered. "Oh, that's the last name, right? We know his last name, and I'll tell it to you. Just as soon as I remember how to spell it. I have to spell it in my mind. It has a *T* in it. I'm just not sure where it goes."

"Well, there are only three families staying with us at this time," he said. "But I cannot tell you their names; it's company policy." He leaned closer and whispered, "But I see that you two are – oh, how should I put this politely? – about as bright as a burnt-out light bulb."

I pretended to look offended. "That's not true. We're ten times brighter than a burnt-out light bulb."

"Exactly! So let's make a game of it, then. I will allow you to guess their last name. It rhymes with mortal."

"Bortle?" I asked. "Does that rhyme with mortal?"

"It does. But it's not their name."

"Vortle, Nortle, Smortal, Gortle, Zortle, Twortle," Cindy rattled off quickly.

"Turtle, is that what you said, young miss? Please stop mumbling."

"Yes, Turtle." Cindy stuck a finger in the air. "That's it! Isn't it?"

"We don't have any turtles here – maybe at the zoo." He paused, perhaps waiting for us to laugh. Cindy and I stared blankly. "We have Tortles, though. And that rhymes with mortal. I believe they are the family you are looking for."

"Yes. They have a kid with them, right?"

"Yes, they have a child. A boy. They are in room 649." He spoke very slowly. "That's Six. Four. Nine." Cindy and I stared blankly again, doing our best impression of simpletons. Cindy didn't have to work as hard at it as I did. "It's on the sixth floor – floor number six. Take the elevator. You press the button to go up."

"Thank you," Cindy said. "I always wondered what those buttons did."

"You're most welcome." He began writing in his ledger.

We went to the elevator. I peered over my shoulder. The night clerk's large eyes followed us. "I have a bad feeling about this." I pressed the button.

"You have a bad feeling about everything," Cindy said.

"I'm usually right, though. That's the problem."

The doors opened. We both took deep breaths and walked in. Hesitantly, palms sweating, I pushed the sixth-floor button. I fully expected the cable to snap, and Cindy and I to end up as preteen pancakes on the floor.

Instead, the elevator rose gently, humming quietly. I breathed in and out several times. "Be ready for anything," I whispered. "Expect the unexpected." Cindy nodded. The doors opened to an empty hallway.

A dark hallway.

My ghost watch detector glowed like a beacon. I reached into my belt pack, retrieved my flashlight, and flicked it on. I stepped off the elevator. Cindy followed.

The doors slammed shut like a snapping mouth.

"EEEYOUCH!" Cindy yelled as she piled into me, knocking us both to the floor. "Holy haddock bones!"

"What is it?" I quickly gained my feet, and swung the flashlight around. Cindy was holding her rear.

"That elevator caught my..." She paused. "Gluteus maximus!"

I laughed. "I can see the headlines: Sidekick's Butt Bit By Evil Elevator! 'That smarts,' the sidekick is quoted." I chuckled uncontrollably. Not a wise move. A good detective should learn to chuckle quietly.

Cindy gave me a shove. "It's not funny! I could have been permanently maimed and forever be known as the dame with the dented derrière. Besides, I'm not a side-kick! How many times do I have to tell you?"

"Can you walk?" I asked.

"Of course!" She gave me another shove. "Let's get on with this."

I pointed my flashlight down the hall. The hall lamps appeared to be in fine shape; they just weren't on.

"Why do you think the lights are out?" I asked.

"Power failure, maybe. They might not have had very good electrical connections back in the thirties."

"Or, does it mean our little ghost is here?" I asked. "That somehow he drained them all."

"He must be here," Cindy said.

We stumbled down the hall, saw that room 649 was the other way. We turned around and walked slowly, side by side, like two cops on patrol. Cindy had her own flashlight out, very much like mine except the plastic covering was pink. We read the numbers: 612, 614, 618. Suddenly they weren't in any order. 635, 624, 619.

"Gasping guppies!" Cindy stared. "Whoever planned out this floor must have been daydreaming."

"Or couldn't count."

We retraced our steps, carefully examining each number. We passed the elevator again and went all the way to the far end of the hallway.

649. The room we wanted.

"Do we knock?" Cindy asked.

"Yes, but again I want you to expect the unexpected."

"You always say that."

"Say what?"

"Expect the unexpected! But if I expect the unexpected it will be expected, so therefore it won't be unexpected any more, so how can I expect it? I'll be busy expecting the expected, and then *bam!* The unexpected will blindside me."

"Huh?" I shook my head. Sidekicks can be so exasperating. "It's easy. Just expect anything, okay?" I spoke slowly. "There could be anything behind this door. Any monstrously ugly and terrible thing."

"I know that. And I'm ready. Stop messing around and let's rock!"

Finally she was speaking my language. I held my flashlight like a billy club and used the butt end to bang against the door: *Knock. Knock. Knock.*

We both took a step back, waited. There could be more ghosts behind the door. Or some evil spectre. Or even some sort of soul-stealing creature. Actually, the more I expected the unexpected, the more I began to sweat.

*Knock. Knock.*

No answer.

*Knock. Knock.*

Our knocking echoed down the dark hallway. Somewhere in the distance the walls creaked, as though the hotel were shifting. Maybe someone was coming from down there. The light above us flickered, crackled and buzzed, then came on. We stared at it. Other lights began glowing, until the hall was suddenly quite well-lit. It was empty.

"Someone found the switch," Cindy said.

I nodded. I did feel better now that there were lights on. I switched my flashlight off. Cindy did the same.

I knocked once more and a door opened.

The one directly behind us.

# CHAPTER FOUR

# NO GIGGLES GILGAMESH

"**A**re you looking for the Tuddles?" a soft male voice asked.

We spun around. A thin gentleman in a long black coat stood there, his face the colour and texture of mottled Swiss cheese. He was so slim he looked like he hadn't had a good meal in a hundred years. He was wearing a top hat, one of those ones you see on Monopoly, and he squinted through a monocle, his one eye bigger than the other.

"Uh, yeah, we were," I said. "Do you know them?"

"I spoke briefly with the Turdles. A charming example of a modern family. Poor Mr. Turdle lost his job in a Regina law office and has been out of work for three years. Three years of wandering around with his family in the Studebaker, taking the odd job here and there. Selling everything they own. But the good news is they're about to start a new life in Saskatoon. He's been awarded a job as a solicitor. A quaint and happy ending, I must say."

"Aren't they the Tortles?" Cindy asked.

"You are correct," the man said. He scratched his chin; his fingernails were long and sharp. "A clever little mousie, aren't you?"

"I'm not little," Cindy corrected. "I'm slightly under-sized, and I don't like being called a –"

He reached towards her. Cindy held still, even her tongue. "Little and shiny as a ruby." With those words he pulled a ruby from behind her ear – or at least that's what it looked like. He held the gem before our wide eyes. It glowed red, a flame burning in the centre. He covered it with his right hand, whispered "Hallazam," and opened his palm. A crimson butterfly took off and flapped in a circle between us. He passed his hand over it, and the butterfly turned into a tiny Chinese fan. He caught it in mid-air and briefly fanned himself. He grinned, displaying small, white teeth.

"A thousand pardons. I have forgotten to introduce myself. I am Baron Roderick Gilgamesh, Lord of Pyrotechnics, Master of Illusions, and King of Ventriloquism."

"He's the Eighth Wonder of the World," a deep voice boomed behind us.

Cindy and I spun around, but the hall was empty. "Who said that?" I asked, but as I turned back, I knew.

Gilgamesh smiled. "It was me. Just a little ventriloquial display." He removed his top hat and bowed deeply, as though he were before a crowd of thousands. He flicked his fingers and presented us each with a ticket. "Complimentary tickets to my performance at the Capitol Theatre. It's on at 8 p.m. Please come. You will witness sights undreamed of."

I looked at my ticket. GILGAMESH THE GREAT, it said on it. *One free admission to this dazzling, pyrotechnic, mesmerizing show.* I pocketed it.

"Thank you, Mr. Gilgamesh," I said. "Very kind of you. We hope to attend. A pleasure to make your acquaintance." That last bit I threw in because I thought it sounded like something they'd say back then.

"Ah, please don't dismiss me yet," Gilgamesh said. "I must repeat my original question: are you looking for the Tortles?"

"Yes, we are," I answered. "Well, we're looking for their son."

"Their son? May I ask why?"

"Uh..." I blanked. The snappy-answers-to-tough-questions part of my brain had shut down completely. "Uh...well..."

"He's my cousin," Cindy finished. "I'm supposed to invite him and his parents to our home for Sunday dinner."

"Oh, what a lovely picture that makes. It appears they're not in." He paused. "I was just about to have some tea, before I go to my performance. Would you do me the favour of joining me?" The door was open a crack. Inside, all I could see was darkness.

And, at the far end of the room, what looked like a small boy sitting in a chair. I squinted. Was it our ghost? The boy was staring at me, his face lit up with a grin. He didn't move though, almost as though he were frozen. His arms hung down at his sides.

He looked smaller than the ghost. Did Gilgamesh have a son?

"Uh, no – no thanks," I said. I had no intention of going in that room with Gilgamesh. Something about him made my flesh creep and crawl. "*The Simpsons* is on TV. We have to get back for it. Right, Cindy?"

"TV?" Gilgamesh's left eyebrow wriggled like a worm above the monocle. "Simpsons? What are you talking about?"

I had forgotten there were no TVs in the 1930s. Oh man, I had to think fast. And hard. "TV. It's like this, uh, pictures in a box that uh, well move, it's new and cool."

"Is it attached to a projector?" he asked.

"It's a type of radio," Cindy said. "With pictures. Like a kaleidoscope."

"Oh, you young children and your programs. I suppose you are fans of *The Shadow?* And decoder rings, too. Very, very exciting! If I see the Tortles, I will inform them that you dropped by."

"Thank you," Cindy said. "We'll leave a note at the desk, too."

The doors to the elevator made a *thunk* as they opened. Gilgamesh stared down the hall, his face turning even paler than Swiss cheese. I glanced over my shoulder, but no one came out of the elevator. The doors closed. When I looked back, Gilgamesh was wiping sweat from his brow. Now, what could frighten him? I wondered.

"It has been a pleasure," he said quickly. "Farewell, dear friends." Gilgamesh bowed and backed into his room. We went as quickly as we could towards the elevators.

"Now he was a weirdo with a capital *W*," Cindy said. "I didn't trust him."

"Me either. Magicians always kind of freak me out. It was almost like he was waiting at that door for us."

"Do you think he can read minds?"

"Absolutely," I said. "I bet all he got when he tried to read your mind was a blank."

She pushed me.

"Let's take the stairs," I said. "I get queasy thinking of the elevator."

"For once I agree with you." We went down the hall, to the door marked Stairs. I pushed it open and suddenly stopped. Cindy stepped on my back heel.

"What are you doing? Let's go."

"Look!" I said.

There were no stairs. It was an empty room. "Do you think they built the stairs later?" I asked.

"That doesn't make sense."

"Maybe they didn't have stairs on this level."

"That must be against the fire code."

"Maybe they didn't have fire codes."

We did an about-face, walked quietly down the hall, and peeked around the corner. Mr. Gilgamesh was gone. Thankfully.

We went to the elevator and pressed the button, watching the metal arrow as it pointed at the first floor, then the second, like a clock. Finally the doors clunked open.

"Girls first," I said.

"Chicken," she muttered and stepped on.

I followed.

The door made a grinding noise when it closed, as though it had jammed shut.

# CHAPTER FIVE

# DON'T ZAP ME!

The elevator hummed and thrummed and whirred downwards, running smoothly and perfectly past floor after floor after floor – my ears popped three times. Four times. Then five.

"Shouldn't we be there by now?" Cindy asked.

"Maybe it's just our imagination," I said, staring at the doors, waiting for them to open.

Instead: down, down, down we went. "Next stop the molten centre of the earth," I joked.

"That's not funny. There's obviously something wrong." She reached towards the buttons. The lights crackled and blinked out.

"Oh great," I moaned. "We're in the dark again."

The elevator suddenly stopped, and I fell to my knees. "Ugh," Cindy said. "Ow."

"Are you okay?" I asked, reaching out. I poked something soft.

"Yeoww!" Cindy yelled. "My eye! Something stabbed my eye! We're not alone in here."

"Uh, it was me."

"Well, I certainly didn't expect that! Watch what you're doing. Maybe get out your flashlight."

I did so, flicked it on. Cindy was cupping her left eye, a look of complete grumpiness polluting her face. "Sorry," I said. "I was only trying to help."

Before she could reply, the elevator shot skyward, gaining speed. It started to pull Gs. My stomach was stuck somewhere below my toes.

"Waalllllltttteerrrrrr!" Cindy said. "Waaaaarrrrrtt!" I pointed the flashlight: her face was beginning to stretch downwards as though it were made of melting wax.

"Woooooow!" I said. My hands were stretching, my fingers as long as ski poles. If I stayed like this, I'd be able to tap someone's shoulder from ten metres away. We were going amazingly fast – maybe we'd break some time/speed warp barrier.

Then – *thunk!* the elevator stopped and our bodies flew up and snapped back into their former shapes and sizes. Gravity yanked us to the floor in a jumble of limbs, aching tendons, stretched muscles, and frazzled nerves. I patted my face to be sure it was normal. Without the slightest fuss, the elevator lights winked back on, and the doors opened.

We tumbled out onto solid ground. Well, carpet anyway. The door closed behind us. We were on the mezzanine floor again. A man in a black suit and red tie walked by, yelling into his cellphone about shares in the Saskatchewan Roughriders.

"We're back," Cindy said. "Creeping catfish! We're back."

I glanced around. Saskatonians and visitors to our fair city were milling about, checking out the gift shop and filing into the restaurant. The opening in the mezzanine floor was just like it was supposed to be – open, that is. It was still nighttime.

"Well, that's a relief!" I said, feeling more than just relieved. Actually, I wanted to run around kissing all the people I saw, I was so happy to be back. But a detective always has to be calm. And I had to set a good example for Cindy. "It appears that your observation is correct," I said, finding just the right tone of authority. My skin was itchy. I scratched my forehead.

"How much time passed?" Cindy asked.

That's supposed to be the first thing you check when you arrive back from time travelling. I looked at my plasmo-watch. "7:43! It's exactly the same time as when we left. Whew! I was worried we'd lose a couple of minutes. Or years."

"Darn, we could have skipped our school years. Well, it's good to be home; that's all I can say. I was worried that time travel would give me jet lag. I'm never going back there."

"Me neither," I said. "At least not today."

"C'mon," she gave me a pull, and I followed her down the stairs. The doorman opened the door for us. "Hope you enjoyed your short stay," he said.

"We sure did," I said. "Best short stay ever!"

Once out on the street I looked over my shoulder at the lights on the Bessborough; the gargoyles and grotesques stared back with stone eyes. There was so much mystery inside that building, I felt myself drawn to it as if it were a magnet and I were a steel ball (with a brain, of course).

"You're not really going back there, are you?"

"Well," I said, "the boy did come and see us at school, right?"

"He just happened to be there."

"And he led us to the Bess. Maybe he needs help. Ghosts don't just hang around for the fun of it. He must have heard how good my – uh, our – detective agency is. I'm sure word has spread all through the afterlife about us. So, I guess in a way he's a client of mine, now. Of ours. And that Gilgamesh guy was a little, well, freaky-deaky, right? I'd like to know more about him."

"You aren't going back," she repeated. She seemed to be stuck in a loop.

"Not alone, I'm not," I said. "Right, partner?"

"Partner! Now you admit that we're partners."

"We haven't failed to solve a case yet," I said.

"We haven't had a case yet!" She rolled her eyes. "Fine! I'll help. But only because I know you'll need it. What do we do first?"

"Gather, identify, solve," I said. "I'll see what I can discover about our little ghost boy."

"Research! I hate research! I'm more into action! Which reminds me, I'm late for tae kwon do class. Let's meet tomorrow night at school. I suppose you'll want to go over plans then."

"You got it. By then I'll have several plans," I said, with all the confidence I could muster. "Maybe even a map or two, also."

She went to her class, and I trotted across the bridge to my house. It's on 12th Street, near Nutana Collegiate, overlooking the river. Our house is a gigantic tan-coloured building – built about eighty years ago, with three floors, twelve rooms, and two kitchens. My room is on the third floor, next to the second kitchen. Which is perfect, because that way I can keep an eye on all of Saskatoon and get a snack whenever I need to. In fact, I have a little balcony just outside my room set up with all my spy stuff. There are about twelve scientific antennae, dishes, and recorders poking up out of the roof. We also have an observatory in the backyard.

"I'm home!" I yelled. "It's me, Walter, your son! I'm home! Don't zap me!"

I have to yell that whenever I open our front door, because, quite frankly, my parents are both mad scientists. Dad has a fear of invading aliens dropping out of the skies, turning humans into plantlike pods, and taking over the world one house at a time. His alien-o-phobia is both a hobby and a full-time occupation.

He once zapped me with a goo gun – several litres of super-sticky, garbage-scented goo that I couldn't get out of my hair for a week. It made me look like a butterfly pupa in a grotesque cocoon. It was the same day as class pictures. Whenever Dad doesn't want to go out and buy me ice cream, I show him the picture.

"It's me! Walter Biggar Bronson! I'm not from Alpha Centauri, nor am I a vampire!"

That last bit was for Mom. She has a doctorate in Psychic and Supernatural Sciences and has developed a phobia about vampires ever since she was attacked by Count Spokula while we were on holiday in Transylvania. He snuck up on her when she was out walking through a misty forest, near our three-star hotel. The count appeared, opened his mouth for a bite, and got the shock of his life – Mom had brought along her holy water mace spray. Mom said he immediately changed into a bat and flapped away, cursing in Transylvanian.

Why a holiday in Transylvania? Cheap flights. My parents may be mad scientists, but they're always fiscally responsible.

Dad was in the living room in his white lab coat, wearing a tinfoil hat. Not just any tinfoil hat, but his specially-folded metallic beanie that blocks his brainwaves from going to Alpha Centauri. Otherwise, the aliens would read his mind all the time. He was also holding a battery-powered buzzer. Two wires led from it to electrodes on his temples.

"Hi, Walter!" He jerked suddenly, as though he'd received a shock.

"What are you doing?"

"Just giving my limbic system a recharge." He jerked again, this time making a weird smiley face. "I'm not quite firing on all synapses this evening. How was your badminton game?"

"We kicked gluteus maximi."

Mom walked in, her dark hair pointing in every direction as though she'd jammed her index finger into a light socket. It was her usual hairstyle. She too wore a white lab coat. "How's my dear little boy?" she asked, kissing my forehead and giving me a squeeze. She smelled like a five-foot-four-inch garlic clove (garlic was her first defence against vampires). After twelve years, I was used to the smell.

"I'm fine; thank you for asking. I've had a very busy day, where I paid attention in every class. We played badminton and beat the Pennock twins."

"Congratulations," Dad said. "They're good players."

"Yep, it felt great. To celebrate, Cindy and I went down to the Bessborough and travelled back in time."

"Oh?" Dad said. He jerked suddenly. "Back in time? Have we given you permission to time travel?"

"Uh, it didn't really come up."

"I don't know if you're old enough to time travel," Mom said.

"There's no age limit."

"Well, you should ask first," Dad added.

"We didn't go on purpose."

"Okay, just be careful," Dad said. "How far back did you go?"

"To 1936."

"Just a jaunt then. You didn't break anything, step on any insects, or attempt to alter the course of the future in any way, shape, or form, did you? You can tell me, son. I won't be mad. Did you?"

"Of course not, Dad. You taught me better than that."

"Did you bring anything home with you?" Mom asked. "You know you're not supposed to do that. Especially people. You didn't bring anyone home, did you? Like a vampire!" She gawked around, clutching at her wooden stake and silver mallet, which always hung on her belt.

"Cancel the red alert, Mom! You know how careful I am. I didn't bring anything home at all." I slid my hand in my pocket. "Uh, I take that back. I did pick up a ticket to a magic show. It's right..." I searched through my pocket. No luck. It had disappeared. When I pulled out my hand, all I had was two blobs of ectoplasm on my finger. "Well, that's funny. A magician handed me a ticket."

"You really shouldn't take things from strangers," Mom said.

"Especially not strangers in the past," Dad added.

I was still staring at the ectoplasm; I had never seen it so thick and green. Mom conjured up a test tube out of her lab jacket, and used a kitchen knife to scrape the goo into the tube. "This is extremely powerful ectoplasm. It has more ectopower than I've ever seen." She held it up so that the kitchen light shone on it. "It wiggles and moves like it's alive. I'll have to test it. I'm going to the synchrotron tomorrow." The synchrotron is at the university. It's a massive machine that takes up a whole Canadian Tire-sized building and produces intense beams of light to view the microstructure of anything. It is kinda like a giant microscope. "I'll be accelerating several different unearthly particles; of course, the university thinks I'm just doing a simple cell test. Maybe I can find out a bit more about this goo."

"I am surprised the tickets disappeared," Dad said. "Objects can hold their corporeal form through time travel. Perhaps it was sleight of hand, and he made it disappear. You can't trust magicians, son. Remember, it's all just visual tricks; they get you looking one way, while the other hand slips the card up a sleeve. There's no such thing as real magicians."

"At least not in this dimension," Mom added.

Dad jerked from another buzz to his limbic system. "Anyway, I'm glad you're back safe and sound. Next time take this with you."

He handed me a rectangular plastic object. I flipped it open. It looked like a Star Trek tricorder.

"What is it?"

"A trans-dimensional, time-travel-proof cellphone. TD2 for short. I will feel a lot better if you take this along with you. Just call us if you need anything. But don't talk long, the charges are abominable."

"Abominable snowman!" Mom echoed. She seemed to snap out of a daze, gawking around the room. "Where?"

Dad ignored her. "This button creates a time field around you and leaves you untouchable. And remember to delouse yourself next time you go on a temporal trip."

"I don't have lice!"

"I'm just saying I don't want you to carry any bugs or disease strains with you."

"We saw a ghost," I said as I Velcroed the phone to my belt.

"A ghost." Mom lifted up her left eyebrow. "What kind of ghost?"

I explained everything, starting with the sighting at Victoria School and ending with me walking in the door to our house.

"Hmmmm," Mom said. Ghosts were more her specialty; Dad didn't find them all that interesting. "It does sound like the little boy is crying out for help. Perhaps something was unsolved in his lifetime. You said wherever he walked, all the lights grew dim?"

"Exactly."

"He certainly has a powerful presence if he can effect that sort of change in the real world. And he can go back and forth in time, apparently. Not every ghost can do that."

42

I suddenly realized one important piece of information: "We didn't actually see him in the past," I said.

"Good observation," Dad said. He grimaced as another bolt of electricity shot into his brain.

"Yes," Mom agreed. "Good thinking. You obviously got that from my side of the family."

Dad rolled his eyes and jerked again. "I think my limbic system is recharged," he announced. "I feel completely brand new."

Mom shook her head. "Good for you. Anyway, this ghost is very curious. Perhaps he guided you to the past. You'll have to figure that out. But you know exactly what to do."

"Gather, identify, solve," we said in unison.

"And have fun," my mother added. She went back to her study.

I climbed up to my room on the third floor and looked across the river to the Bessborough. It appeared and disappeared in the falling snow, as though the whole building were playing a trick on my brain. What would my next step be? Even though I have trained my mind to be an ultra-supersonic logic machine, it sometimes doesn't work: I couldn't think of a plan. Maybe I needed to borrow my father's limbic recharging device.

But I already had a system to help recharge my brain – a Nintendo system. I played a game that featured Indiana Jones running through a temple, avoiding rolling rocks and solving puzzles. And suddenly, while I was trying to jump from a rock to a swinging rope, I paused in mid-air. Paused the game, that is.

The answer came to me, and a plan formed in my mind. I knew what I'd do tomorrow.

CHAPTER SIX

# GHOSTS? LET ME TELL YOU ABOUT 'EM.

hosts are absolutely and completely logical. I know, sometimes they scream and scare the pants off people, but they always have a reason for it. If someone was murdered most foully in a chicken coop, they would most likely haunt that chicken coop.

So why had this ghost come up and tapped me on the shoulder? He had specifically appeared at Victoria School and had intended for us to follow him to the Bessborough. That would suggest that he had a connection with both buildings. Why else would he be travelling between them?

This was my first big case, and I didn't want to mess

it up – I was sure there would be plenty more. The main reason this time travel and ghostly otherworld stuff happens is because I live in Saskatoon. The problem with Saskatoon is that no one believes it exists. Oh sure, the people who live here, Saskatonians (or Saskatoonians or Tooners), they *know* the place is real, but step outside the city limits and no one believes there is, or ever was, such a place as Saskatoon.

"Didn't it sink into the sea?" they say. "Was that the capital of Atlantis? Or was it covered by a volcano?" The Prime Minister never visits. The Queen was here once, but no one believes that. "Who in their right mind would name their city after a purple berry?"

Saskatoon is the Bermuda Triangle of the prairies. It's also the ghost capital of Canada. People complain about ghosts in their cellars, popping up their laundry chutes, starting their lawnmowers at night (but never cutting the lawn, they're lazy ghosts), taking cabs and paying in old money that disappears seconds later. They even stride along the Meewasin Trail and tap couples on the back just as they're about to kiss.

Hey, I'm not complaining – ghosts are good for business. Once I solved this mystery, I'd make the front page of *The StarPhoenix*, and my phone would be ringing off the hook with calls from little old ladies wanting to get the ghosts out of their pianos, mechanics trying to find the ghosts in their machines.

Anyway, I *had* to solve this case. So I did the only logical thing I could think of – I decided to sneak a look at the principal's files. Who knew, I might even ask first. I'm not completely crazy, and I never break the rules unless it's absolutely necessary to crack a case.

The next day, during second period, I walked into the secretary's office and announced, "Hello, I'm Walter Biggar Bronson, private detective." I flipped my card towards her like a ninja throwing a shuriken.

Miss Stang caught it between two fingers and dropped it to the desk. She had lightning-quick reactions and was an equally fast thinker. Many students have tried to pull the wool over the Sphinx. I call her that because she sits at her desk watching everything, measuring all.

"I know who you are, Walt," Miss Stang said, her voice rumbling like a bullhorn. "Nearly every day I sign you in late." She rubbed a hand through her short, spiky hair.

"I apologize profusely for my tardiness." I hoped my big words would confuse her, or at least make her give me the respect I was due. "I always have a valid excuse, do I not?"

"You live two blocks from school. There are no excuses." This conversation was heading entirely in the wrong direction. A little misdirection was needed.

"May I see the personal files of all students from 1936?"

"No, you may not. Where do you come up with these requests? Files are confidential." She paused and fixed me with a hard, sphinxy stare. "You know what that means – you aren't supposed to look at them."

"I understand, and I'm absolutely sorry. I realize the error of my ways. You are completely correct, Miss Stang. I shall leave right now. In fact, I will go at once."

And I promptly turned on my heel and left. Well, the head-on approach didn't work. It was time for Operation Change-My-Voice. I darted into the staff room, and looked left and right. Empty. All the teachers must be out golfing, marking papers, or cackling in their classrooms as they made up impossibly hard pop quizzes. I dialed the front desk and set the voice modulator on my watch to make it sound like I was a really old male – late thirties at least.

"Victoria School," Miss Stang answered.

"Hello! This is Mr. – Uh – Zigglebottom." Why didn't I think of a name beforehand? "We need you in the gym."

"Mr. Who?"

"Zigglebottom." Great. I had picked the stupidest name in the universe. My plan was going to fail. I decided to try anyway. "But that's not important. What is important is this: we need you right here, right now."

"For what?"

"It's a..." My brain froze. "Uh..." It was never going to thaw. "Uh...a wild gopher emergency! Get down here immediately. That's an order!" I hung up.

Okay, maybe I need a bit of work on my improv skills, but 2.5 seconds later Miss Stang roared past the door.

So I snuck into the principal's office.

Principal Robert Pytlowany is a highly organized, efficient man who collects toy trains. His office looked like a miniature train station. There were engines and cars everywhere, hanging from strings, pictured in post-cards and paintings. Tracks ran from the desk to his garbage can – in fact, he had a special trash train that dumped its load into the bin. His pen holder was a giant caboose.

I walked carefully to the file cabinet, trying not to bump into any suspended tracks. I flicked the motion detector on my watch, which beeps as people approach. It was silent – so there no one within fifteen metres.

I flipped through the files. The first thing that caught my eye was a file from 1962 that was sticking out farther than the others. It was for Janet McGaffin. Inside were her marks, a picture, and a clipping from *The*

*StarPhoenix* titled: *Students Claim They Travelled in Time.*

> Janet McGaffin and John Williams, two seventh
> grade students from Victoria school, stumbled into
> the Saskatoon police station with the strangest tale.
> They claimed they travelled back in time, were kid-
> napped by a sinister being, attacked by a horribly
> scary monster, and locked in a trunk. According to
> them, all this happened at the Bessborough Hotel.
> Their parents say the two children have extremely
> active imaginations and that a good rest, a prohibi-
> tion on candy, and a couple weeks away from the
> Capitol Theatre would be helpful for them.

This was an amazing story. And it had to be true. It
looked like Cindy and I weren't the first to go back in
time. I wondered if Janet and John still lived in
Saskatoon; I would have to interview them. I memo-
rized their names and slid the file closed.

Speaking of time, I didn't have much. So I quickly
continued flipping – 1942, 1939, then 1936. There were
editions of the old school newspaper. Report cards. A
letter from the Prime Minister saying he refused to
sanction the school as a royal school because he didn't
believe that Saskatoon existed.

Then, finally: Tortle, Archibald E.

It was the only Tortle; it had to be our ghost. Born in Maple Creek in 1928, mother and father Roland and Allison Tortle. He'd enrolled January 22nd, 1936.

The only other item in his file was a small card that had a drawing of a dove on the front. I opened it: a funeral announcement dated February 17th, 1936. For Roland, Allison, and Archibald Tortle.

Oh, how awful, I thought. Three deaths at once. The poor family. I wondered what had happened. Obviously it had to be terrible. Otherwise, why would Archibald still be wandering around?

Suddenly the motion detector on my watch started beeping. Loud. I slapped the file shut and ducked between the cabinet and the wall.

In lumbered Principal Pytlowany. I could tell because his shoes were extra big and had a very particular *clomp* to them. He sat at his desk and hummed to himself, opening and closing drawers. "Choo Choo," he said. I peeked around the corner. He was pushing a train across his desk. "Wave to the caboose driver. Wave. Here comes the eleven o'clock." He let out his breath. "Ah.... I miss the good ol' days when things were simple. No patrolling, no teachers to organize, no detentions to give. Just pop quizzes and school trips. If only I was an engineer. Choo, Choo."

I needed a diversion. Just a few centimetres from my

feet was a wooden train with a golden key protruding from its smokestack. I slowly wound the key and released the train.

"*Hooot! Hooot!*" its whistle blew the second I let it go.

"What!" Principal Pytlowany exclaimed. I heard him scramble around the desk. "My little steam engine – the one that could – what set you off?"

I peeked again. He had his back turned as he picked up the train and examined it.

I dashed out, with all the finesse of James Bond.

And ran smack dab into Miss Stang.

CHAPTER SEVEN

# INSIDE SASKATOON'S CEREBRAL CORTEX

"Walter Bronson, what are you doing?" Her hand clamped onto my shoulder like a vice. She had long nails – five of them, each leaving its own indentation in my flesh.

"Fire drill," I said.

"Excuse me?"

I scrambled my brains trying to find a good excuse. "Just practising in case there's a fire drill."

"First, you don't run during a fire. And secondly, what were you doing in Mr. Pytlowany's office?"

"Who was in my office?" Principal Pytlowany was behind me now, clutching the train. I was caught between them, looking back and forth. Miss Stang stared down, her eyes angry, stony, and cold. Those eyes could read my mind. "Tell us what you were doing," she said. "Right now. Or do you want me to guess? Because I'm a great guesser."

A good detective knows when to spill the beans. "I was in your office, sir."

"Why?"

"I was looking at your trains, Mr. Pytlowany. They're wonderful, sir."

"Thank you, they are, aren't they?" He smiled, then shook his head. "Still, you shouldn't be in my office without me around. You know better than that."

"I do, sir. I mean, I should, sir."

Miss Stang nudged me. "You have more to tell us, don't you? Things will go better for you if you come clean."

"Oh, uh, yeah, I should also point out that I was looking at the files."

"You what!" Principal Pytlowany exclaimed. "Those are confidential."

"I know, sir. I just..." and here I had a dilemma. I couldn't tell them about the ghost; that would open up a whole new can of afterlife worms. Most adults don't believe in ghosts. "I was doing a history study. I'm just interested in the school in the 1930s. You know, what they used to call the Dirty Thirties." I threw that last line in to prove I was paying attention in class.

"You still shouldn't be looking at the files without permission. You understand that, don't you? You will have to be punished."

"I would have been here," Miss Stang said, "but someone called in a gopher emergency at the gym."

"A what?"

"A gopher emergency! It was Mr. Zigglebottom – whoever that is. It was all a trick."

"Who do you think did it?" the principal asked.

She narrowed her eyebrows. "I think it was an inside job, someone from the school. I'll get to the bottom of this."

Uh-oh. They might somehow figure out it was me. "Uh, may I suggest a punishment, sir? For me, that is?"

"You may," Principal Pytlowany said.

"I'll write an extra paper. Say...about Saskatoon's history. Will that be a good punishment?"

"Yes. Perfectly suitable. Get to work on it immediately. It will be five pages long, and I expect to see it on my desk tomorrow morning."

My eyes widened. "Tomorrow morning! But –"

"No buts. You'll have to get it done."

"I'll need outside sources – we don't have the right

books in our library. It might require a trip to the Frances Morrison Library to visit the Local History Room."

"Yes. That will be fine. You have my permission to visit the library downtown. But..." He took a step closer and glared down at me. I began to sweat. What did he want? Did he know something about the gopher emergency – should I confess that, too? The light above him bored into my eyes. "You look a little too smug, Mr. Bronson. Perhaps you're hiding something else. So I will double the length of that paper to ten pages. You may begin working on it now. Remember, you won't get away with things on my watch." He turned to Miss Stang. "Now tell me about this gopher emergency."

I slipped away.

Half an hour later, I was downtown, pushing my way through the turnstile into the Frances Morrison Library. I climbed to the second floor (avoiding the elevator, I was quickly developing a phobia), went past the rows of CDs, videocassettes, and DVDs, and into the Local History Room.

The LHR is just like the memory cortex of the human brain – no, it's not grey and mushy, that's not what I mean. It's where all the memories of Saskatoon are stored. There are several archivists who, like worker ants, go out and collect bits and pieces of our history and bring it back here to be carefully filed.

"Hello, Walter," Miss Schaefer said. She was the head archivist, a youthful woman who had a mind more powerful than a massive computer. She knew me well from all my investigations; so well, in fact, that she allowed me to call her by her first name, Laureen. A good detective knows how to make good contacts. I also bring her chocolates every second visit. "Busy saving the universe today?" she asked.

"I have never purported to save the universe," I answered. "Just to solve a few mysteries, send a few bogeymen back to their proper dimension, and dissuade the occasional werewolf from setting up camp down by the weir. At least those are some of my long-term goals."

"Oh, I see. How can I help you today?"

"I'm curious about any deaths that happened in 1936. The specific accident I'm interested in involved the Tortle family. Did anything terrible happen that year?"

Laureen smiled. "Ah, kids today. You never change. Always interested in the gruesome and grotesque. I'll bring you a file of *The StarPhoenix* from 1936 – it was the middle of the Depression, so I'm sure there will be lots of pieces about falling wheat prices. Any particular month?"

"February."

"I may be a while. You might want to occupy your time reading a book. They're Vitamin A for your brain."

She was always saying things like that. I remembered my report, so I went to the computer, punched in the words "Saskatoon History" and came up with several different books. I found the largest one, took it off the shelf and went back to the LHR. I rediscovered some things I already knew, that our fair city was named after a Cree word for a saskatoon berry and was originally formed from a Temperance colony in 1883 – Temperance people were the ones who were against drinking, swearing, or anything, well, intemperate. People liked the area, kept moving here, and in 1901 it became a village, in 1903 blossomed into a town, and by 1905 had hustled and bustled its way into being a city – a boom town. Which doesn't mean it exploded, just that the population grew. I knew all about the boomtown years because Mom had lots of stories involving the boomtown ghosts who were still hanging around. That's one thing the historians miss – how many ghosts per capita hang out in Saskatoon.

I flipped ahead and found an article about the Bessborough. This was doubly good; it would help both my assignment and my case. I knew Archibald probably hung around the Victoria School because that's where he'd attended class. But why the

Bessborough? It was built by the Canadian National Railway in the 1930s, had over 200 rooms and was twelve storeys high. And it was named after the Earl of Bessborough, Mr. Ponsonby, who was the Governor General of Canada at the time. So that explained the funky name. The hotel was finished in 1931 but stood empty for four years because it was too expensive to furnish. That was weird; then suddenly the answer hit me. No one had any money in the Depression. So that's why they didn't buy furniture. A detective always has to have his brain clicking. The Bess finally opened in 1935. The Tortles had obviously stayed there only a few months after the grand opening. I jotted down several notes, planning on using them later for my paper.

Laureen returned and dropped a thick file in front of me. Dust swirled up around it. "Careful," she said. "Some of that dust is from the Dirty Thirties. Get it?"

"Ha, ha!" I said. "I get it. Ho, ho!" I should point out that librarians have rather interesting senses of humour. It's best to laugh when they make a joke, even if you're not sure what it means.

She next handed me a pair of white gloves. "You know the drill."

I donned the gloves, feeling a little funny, but it was to prevent my finger oils from getting onto the paper and causing it to disintegrate. "Have fun," she said over her shoulder. "Don't get lost in the past."

Good advice. I should have it printed on a T-shirt. On the back it would say: "And watch out for vampires!"

I flipped through the pages, looking at the dates, slowing as I reached February. There was a piece about William Hopkins, the Saskatoon mayor who had died that month. I turned the page and my heart stopped.

Gilgamesh's bodiless head floated before me, staring, his hands reaching out. He was part of a half-page ad, but it was so well drawn that he momentarily appeared real. "SPELLBINDING! AN ABSOLUTELY AMAZING SHOW OF MESMERISM, MAGIC, AND VENTRILOQUISM. 8:00 P.M. ARRIVE EARLY, LEAVE FULL OF WONDER." I had met him in the flesh, and here it was – proof that he had really existed. I got that sudden exciting thrill – a thrill that only comes as clues fall into place. The case was getting closer to being solved.

I slowly turned a few more pages until I reached February 14th. On the front page I found two stark black-and-white photographs. The first was of a Studebaker that had broken through the frozen river; only the back end was visible, poking out of a hole in the ice. The second photograph was of a pale, unconscious boy in a hospital bed, nurses and a doctor at his side. The article below them read:

## PARENTS DIE IN ICY MISHAP!
## BOY NEAR DEATH IN HOSPITAL!

A dramatic and sad story unfolded on the back roads near Saskatoon last night. Mr. Roland Tortle and his wife and child went out for a drive and attempted to take a shortcut over the frozen South Saskatchewan river at around 8:00 p.m. Due to the recent thaw, the ice broke and the Studebaker plunged into the freezing water. Charles Buitenhuis, an off-duty police officer who was ice fishing nearby, pulled all three Tortles from the sunken automobile. His valiant effort wasn't rewarded. Mr. and Mrs. Tortle died on the scene. Their son survived and was brought to City Hospital, but is in critical condition. Roland Tortle had three tickets to Gilgamesh the Great's sold-out performance, so police believe they may have been in a hurry to return for the show, and mistakenly took the closed ice road. Mr. Tortle was scheduled to start employment today as a barrister with Gimford and Associates.

There it was. The poor parents, newly arrived from southern Saskatchewan, had died tragically. And on an unlucky February 13th. They must have been staying at the hotel because they had no home. And Mr. Tortle had found a job, even though it was the Depression.

They perhaps even celebrated with dinner, then went out for a drive. One wrong turn and a few seconds later it was all over.

But what had happened to Archie? I flipped to the next day's paper and the headline read:

### TORTLE BOY PASSES AWAY
### AFTER TERRIBLE ACCIDENT!

Archibald Tortle, who was rescued from the freezing South Saskatchewan waters on February 13th, passed away only moments after learning the news of his parents' death. Medical staff had chosen not to tell him about his parents' fate, but when he awoke he asked to see the cartoons in the paper, and was able to read the headline and see the photograph of the Studebaker stuck in the broken ice. Nurses say he whispered his parents' names and a few minutes later died. Doctors are unable to say the exact cause of death, although they are suggesting it might be hypothermia.

The poor, unlucky boy. No wonder he looked so sad. He probably had only just learned to read. But this wasn't a murder mystery. The real mystery was, why was Archibald haunting the area? He had somehow made us time travel back to February 13, 1936, the day he died.

What else had happened? Was there something more? I couldn't help thinking of Gilgamesh. Somehow there had to be a connection. Though I had nothing to link the two events, it did seem as though Archie had led us right to Gilgamesh.

Or was it a coincidence?

A shadow fell across me. "Did you find more stuff, Laureen?" I asked.

A book thumped on the table. I gently closed the file. The book was *The Wonderful Wizard of Oz*. I looked up. It wasn't Laureen staring down, but some other librarian. She had grey-and-whitish hair tied in a bun; her wrinkles spread out from around her eyes, as though they had formed from squinting at too many books. She probably should have retired a few years ago. Her name tag read Janet McGaffin.

"You are Walter Bronson, aren't you?"

"Yes," I said. She looked familiar; I was in the library so often that I'd seen her several times, but had never spoken to her.

"Have you read this book? It's a very important book. Every child should read it. That's what I think."

She was going batty, that was my first impression. It happens to every librarian eventually – it's some kind of reaction to reading so many books in one lifetime. "I have read it, yes. And seen the movie, too."

"What is it about?" she asked quickly, her voice tense. "Quick, tell me. Right now!"

I glanced around. She wasn't just batty, she was bonkers. There wasn't another librarian in sight. "Uh... it's about a girl named Dorothy and her dog Toto, and they, umm, travel to Oz on a tornado –"

"It's a cyclone," the librarian interrupted. "Cyclone! Remember that! Now, carry on!"

"Uh, then Dorothy meets a lion and a tin guy and a scarecrow, and they kill the Wicked Witch of the West, and Dorothy taps her red magic shoes at the end, saying, 'There's no place like home, there's no place like home.' And suddenly she's home."

"Good," she said. "Good! Except in the book the shoes are silver, and she says, 'Take me home to Aunt Em!' Otherwise you did just fine. It's important that you know it. Very important."

I looked at her tag again, so I could remember who she was when I told Laureen about this incident. When I read her name a second time, I froze.

"You're Janet McGaffin," I said. I had just read a clipping about her this morning. "You and John Williams went back in time in 1962. In the Bessborough. You told the police, but no one believed you."

"No, they didn't," she said, almost sadly. "No one believed us. They teased us all the time. Even when we

were older. John moved to Montreal. I became a librarian."
She paused. "Librarians never tease you about stories."

"What happened to you? What did you see?"

She smiled. "I can't tell you. If I tell you, things might
not happen in the same way. I've read every time-travel
book ever written. I know the rules."

"Then why did you want me to see this book?"

"I wanted to be sure you had read it, that's all."

"Is there something in it I need to know?"

"It will help you, I think. You're a good boy. A smart
boy. You should be going now."

"But wait, can't you tell me anything?"

"Yes," she paused, and smiled sweetly. She looked ten
years younger. "Thank you. I've been waiting to say that
for a long time. Thank you for everything." She turned
away.

Why was she thanking me? I hadn't done anything.
I watched her until she disappeared behind a shelf of
books. Maybe every answer I was looking for was right
there in her brain. But she couldn't tell me one single
thing.

Which meant it was time to do a bit more footwork.

# CHAPTER EIGHT

# FROM ONE MESS
# TO ANOTHER

I met Cindy at Victoria school at 7:20 that evening. Our plan was to wait by the lockers until Archie returned. I was pretty sure he'd be drawn back to this place – he wanted us to find him. Several badminton players strode by us, and my palm began itching to hold a racquet. The Pennock twins didn't even look our way. Guess they held a bit of a grudge. "Have a good practice," Cindy yelled.

When the hall was clear, I told her everything I'd figured out.

"The poor family," she said. "It's so unfair. Everything was finally going their way."

"It is terrible. But we have to remember it happened

a long time ago. Although for little Archie it probably seems like yesterday."

Kelly, the janitor, strode by carrying a mop. He glanced suspiciously our way, as though he thought we'd made the mess he was about to clean up. He was probably mad at me for that ectoplasm experiment I'd once tried in the gym. The green stains still hadn't come out of the curtain.

Seeing the mop reminded me of the maids in the Bessborough. They had looked like twins. I'd have to check them closely when we went back. Of course, after awhile, I suppose everyone in the past looks the same.

"What time is it?" Cindy asked.

"Time for you to get a watch," I said. And I meant it. She hadn't worn a watch for ages; she felt it slowed down her reflexes. "It's 7:45," I added.

"It looks like Archie's a no-show," she said. "He was here by 7:30 yesterday."

"He'll come back, I'm sure of it," I said, feeling completely unsure. Another thing I'd read about ghosts is that they are absolutely undependable. "He has to. We haven't discovered his secret."

"You still think it was this Gilgamesh?" she asked.

"It's just a hunch."

"Like that hunch you had that there wouldn't be a snap Social Studies test last week?"

"So my hunches aren't always right."

"Well, in between sit-ups and crunches, I did some more research on the Internet about Gilgamesh," she said. "He was only here for three nights. He came from Germany and toured all of North America. Creepy as he was, I don't know what he would have to do with the Tortles' accident."

"Maybe he hypnotized them," I said.

"Why?"

"I don't know. To try to get them to come to his show? Maybe that's what Archie wants us to discover. When he shows up."

"*If* he shows – there he is!"

As if on cue, the lights dimmed at the far end of the hallway. Archie stood there staring at us, mouthing words. We walked towards him. He somehow looked even sadder today, as though all the memories of death and mourning were pressing down on him. Ghosts don't need sleep, but he looked like a boy who hadn't slept for seventy years. When we got closer, he slowly turned around, and we followed.

"He's taking exactly the same path as last night," I said. We crossed the bridge and went down to Spadina. A minute later the doorman opened the door, stepped out, and looked around. While he was still glancing around, Archie went in.

"Why does he wait for the doorman?" Cindy asked.

"Hard to say," I answered. As the CEO of the detective agency, it was my job to have answers, so I came up with one. "Maybe the first time he went into the hotel in real life a doorman opened the door. And he just likes that feeling. He's still a kid at heart, remember."

"You two again," the doorman said. He scratched his head, still holding the door open. "Is there someone else with you? A little boy?"

"You saw someone else?" I asked.

"Yes. A young boy. He seemed really sad. My heart went out to him."

So even the untrained eye could see Archie. The stronger the ghost, the more people he appears to. Ghosts vibrate slightly in the afterlife dimension, so you have to adjust your eyes. It was making me a little cross-eyed, though.

"I must be imagining things," he said. "Right?"

Most people don't want the existence of ghosts confirmed. "It does sound very peculiar," I said. "Thank you for opening the door for us. You're doing a wonderful job." We went up the stairs. The elevator doors closed across the hall. We watched the lights.

"It's stopping at the fifth floor," Cindy said. "Just like last night."

The fourth floor and the sixth lit up at the same

time. The light made a *zap* noise and conked out.

"What does that mean?" I asked. "It's like we're repeating the same code."

We got on the other elevator.

"Now, we should be careful," I said. "Do you remember exactly what you did to send us to the past last time?"

"No! Do you?"

"Me? You're the sidekick; you're supposed to take notes. I can't believe you didn't even note it. Why do you think I gave you that digital recorder?"

She pulled the wafer-thin recorder out of her pocket and spoke into the tiny microphone. "Note to self: Walter is a pig-headed nerd." She slipped it back.

"Hey!" I said. "That's rude! And untrue."

"Stop calling me a sidekick. Would a sidekick do this?" She punched the fifth floor button, then jammed the fourth and sixth floor buttons at the same time. "There! I think that's the right combo."

"Either that, or we're going to experience a big surprise."

The elevator shot up to the fifth floor and stopped. The cables rattled, and it dropped down to the fourth floor, thudding to a stop. After a moment's pause it fell again. I felt dizzy, disoriented, and droopy.

"I wish I had some ginger ale," I said. "That always settles my stomach."

The doors opened, and a man in a fedora stepped in. He tipped his hat towards us. "Evening, kiddos," he said.

"Good evening!" we said in unison. We stepped out. It was the mezzanine from 1936. The same desk clerk was on duty.

Cindy rubbed her hands together. "See, that was easy."

"Lucky guess," I said. I looked at the calendar. The date was now February 14th, 1936. The clock on the wall showed that it was just after 8:00 p.m. A full day had passed since the last time we were here.

"That's the day after his parents died," I said. "Archie spent the whole day in the hospital, so we might not find him here."

"We just saw his ghost walk upstairs. So there must be something here he wants us to see."

"Your deductive powers are getting better," I said. "I'm proud of you."

A bellboy walked by, in a red uniform with a round red pillbox cap.

"Poor guy," Cindy whispered.

"Why?"

"They have to wear such cheesy hats. You couldn't pay me enough to wear a hat like that."

"Will you concentrate on the task at hand?" I said. "This isn't a fashion study."

The desk clerk looked up. His eyes narrowed. He obviously remembered us from our last visit. He tapped a pencil on his desk.

"What do you want to do?" Cindy asked.

"Well, first let's get away from the desk clerk – he keeps staring at us." I took her by the shoulder, and we slipped into a room that turned out to be a library. There was a hotel guest in there wearing a fedora, reading *The Saskatoon StarPhoenix*. The shelves were stacked with books.

"So this is what people did before they had TV," Cindy said. "Came down here and read."

"Primitive, isn't it?" I said. I perused the shelves. "And boring," I added.

"Boring?" Cindy said. "I thought you liked reading."

"I love it." I pulled a book off the shelf. *The Wonderful Wizard of Oz*. "Just not the same book over and over again."

"What?" She looked at the shelf. "They *are* all the same." Every book was *The Wonderful Wizard of Oz*. "What a cheap hotel. That's like getting cable TV and having the same program on every channel."

"It *is* rather odd. And this is the same book that Janet McGaffin showed me in the library." I opened the book, read a little bit about the cyclone lifting up Dorothy's house. I flipped ahead, finding the part where the winged monkeys attack Dorothy and her crew. No help to me. I closed the covers. "I wish she'd told me why I should know this book." I set the copy back on the shelf. "It's not like I have time to reread it now. I do have a plan, though."

I told her my plan.

"Why does your plan always involve the elevator?"

"Because apparently there aren't any stairs."

"And your plans always involve breaking into something."

"That's what detectives do."

"Let's go then. But next time I get to think up the plan."

We went into the elevator and pressed the sixth-floor button. The elevator clanked and hummed, rose up, up, and stopped. The doors opened. The hallway was dimly lit, light dappling down across us.

"You first," she said. "It's your plan."

We went left, reading the numbers which still weren't in numerical order. Something about that bothered me. This was one of the classiest hotels in the west. They knew how to count. So why were the numbers out of order? How would guests find their rooms?

We came to 649. There was no light below the door, just as I expected. So I turned to Gilgamesh's room. According to the ad his show was at 8:00 p.m.; therefore, he would be gone. I knocked. No answer. When I knocked again, the door budged a little. I pushed it a little farther, peeked through the crack. There was a dim light, but I couldn't make out much more than an empty wooden chair.

"You can't just barge in," Cindy whispered.

"Well, what do you suggest we do? We don't have long until he's back."

"Just pretend you're a bellboy."

"Good idea," I whispered. "Room service!" I said. "Room service."

My voice echoed.

The door creaked as I pushed it open, squeaking like an angry bat. The hairs on the back of my neck poked straight up, and every nerve ending in my body stood at attention. I was ready for anything. Especially turning tail and running.

I took a slow and extremely cautious step inside. Then another. Cindy was a few centimetres behind me, her nasal breathing echoing in my ears. My eyes adjusted to the dimness. There was a mess of brown paper wrapping in the corner. Several cloaks were strewn across the floor near a writing desk.

"He's not all that neat," Cindy said.

"Maybe he was in a hurry." I crept to the middle of the room.

Something rustled, but it was such a small noise I wasn't sure where it came from.

"What was that?" Cindy asked.

"Mice," I said. "I hope."

"How would mice get to the sixth floor?"

"On the elevator, silly. They'd stand on each other's shoulders and press the buttons." This was something I had worked hard at – being funny under extreme duress. Cool, hip, and funny, no matter how scared I was.

We rounded the corner. An electric lamp flickered on the bedside table, beside a big black phone. The bed was made perfectly, but scattered around it were hundreds of peacock feathers, silk and gold outfits for Gilgamesh's show, three large swami hats, and a huge pile of discarded clothes and sheets.

"Help me," whispered a tiny voice.

We both froze, doing our impression of ice statues.

"Help me," the voice whispered from beneath the pile. "Helllp!"

CHAPTER NINE

# TOOTHPICK FACE

The pile of clothes moved. "Plllleassse, hellllp me."

Cindy's face was side-swiped by a look of fear – the same look that was probably on my face.

"Should we?" she asked.

"It could be a trap."

"Hellllpp meeee."

The voice sounded absolutely pathetic.

"Okay, let's do it," I decided. "But expect the – well, just be ready." I leaned down and pulled off one of the robes. "Archie?" I asked, a gut reaction. But the voice was silent now. I hoped he hadn't smothered. I worked faster. Several robes, two towels, and one sheet later I found a small foot in a dark brown shoe. The leg kicked. I yanked back two more robes and a small hand appeared.

It was clenched in a fist. I ripped away the final robe.

A small boy stared up at us, his odd, large eyes wide open, his face missing a chunk of flesh.

Horrified, I looked closer. I was wrong. He wasn't missing a chunk from his cheek; it was more like he'd been chipped. His face was carved from wood. His eyes were two ping-pong balls.

"Bagpiping blackfish! It's a ventriloquist's dummy!" Cindy said. She assumed a defensive stance and snapped her head left and right. "Gilgamesh is here! He must be in the room right now, throwing his voice."

I glanced around. No sudden shadows leapt from behind the door, no dark figures jumped out of the bathroom. In fact, the room was eerily silent, except for my wheezy breathing.

I looked back at the dummy. His left cheek had been cracked as though he'd been hit with a hammer.

"The room seems to be empty," I said.

"Who were we hearing?" Cindy asked.

"Me, dummy," the dummy said. His eyes swivelled in their sockets, looking from Cindy to me. He stuck out his wooden tongue.

I leapt back.

"Didn't mean to scare you," he said, pulling his tongue back in. "I was just tired of suffocating under all those robes. Well, not that I *can* suffocate, but I was feeling claustrophobic." He rolled his eyes to Cindy. "That's a big word, isn't it, girlie? It means afraid of enclosed spaces."

Cindy was in her tae kwon do stance. "He's got to be here somewhere. Show yourself, Gilgamesh!"

"He's gone," the dummy said. "Mr. Grand Poobah is off doing his show. He abandoned me." The voice did seem to be coming from the dummy. He raised his eyebrows. "Don't be so jumpy, chumps."

"You're...you're talking," I said.

"You're surprised? Haven't you heard of a talking dummy? We're very commonplace. That's why they call me Billy the Talking Boy."

"We're talking to a dummy," Cindy said. She had moved closer and was looking down at him. "But dummies can't talk."

"You're talking, isn't that proof enough?" Billy said.

Cindy narrowed her eyebrows. I'd seen this look before; she was only one iota away from unleashing a snap kick.

"Who's your sidekick?" Billy asked me. "Hey cutie! You don't have much going on upstairs, do you?"

"What!" she pulled back her left leg, and thrust it quickly downward.

"Whoa! Hold up!" He raised his hands. Cindy stopped her foot a centimetre from his chest. "You're the one who called *me* a dummy. Don't let her get me, boss. I'm made of the finest basswood, and I'm too young for the toothpick factory."

"The fact that he can talk could be some kind of ghost effect," I said. "Or a psychic energy surge that's somehow filtering through this dummy – uh, wooden toy."

"Or I could be a talking dummy. Bad enough Gilgy-boy abandons me and takes Mr. Fancy Pants to replace me – but you two don't even believe I'm real."

"I think you're real," I said. I was pretty sure Gilgamesh wasn't here. "I don't know how you're talking, but I've heard of stranger things."

"Well, that makes me feel better." He rubbed his forehead, getting rid of imaginary sweat. "I'm tired of staring at the ceiling. Would you kindly put me in that chair over there?"

"Be careful," Cindy said.

He stuck his tongue out towards her. "I don't bite, boss."

I picked him up, surprised at how heavy he was. "I want to be a real boy, just like you, Geppetto," he said, winking.

"You're not Pinocchio," I pointed out. "Does your nose grow when you lie?"

"I never lie," he answered as I sat him in the chair.

"Ah, that's much better. Ol' Gilgy knows I hate the floor. He's such a bully – he's always yanking my chain."

Cindy laughed.

"It's not funny. How'd you like your mouth to open every time someone pulls a string? And look at these clothes. Yechh! Not dapper! Not stylish! Then one day Woody, his parrot, attacks me, takes a chip out of my face, and Gilgamesh doesn't fix me. Some kids even called me Splinterface. It still hurts to think of it." His face clouding over with emotion, he looked as sad as Archie.

I had no idea how to comfort a depressed dummy. So I switched topics. "Do you know anything about the family next door? The Tortles?"

"Poor family." Billy's eyelids dropped closed and opened again. "Doomed, that's what they were. Doomed. You could feel it on them a mile away. Gilgamesh took a special interest in them."

"What kind of interest?" I asked.

"He gave them free tickets to the show. Told them to come no matter what. He knew they were fated to die. He can see things. He tried to save them."

"He did?" Cindy asked.

"Yes. He may be overbearing, arrogant, and a complete cad, but he's not evil. He just pretends to be mystifying and terrible. It's part of his act, and it's what people want to see. I'll tell you a little secret about Gilgamesh. He's petrified."

"Petrified?" I asked. "What could possibly frighten Gilgamesh?"

Billy looked around. His ping-pong-ball eyes grew wide with fear. "Eih Cra," he whispered. The name echoed through the room like a death rattle.

"What? Who? Huh?" I whispered back.

Billy pointed up and all around him. "We've been here in this hotel for days – too many days. At night there are odd noises – crying, moaning, screaming. And something that sounds like a giant hyena. But it's more than just sounds. Eih Cra is the one who's pulling the strings here."

"The hotel manager?" Cindy asked.

Billy laughed. "Did you get her at a discount? No. I said..." He paused. "Eih Cra. Gilgamesh thinks there's an extremely powerful supernatural presence in this hotel. He wants to get away from it. We try to leave, but we always end up here. It's as if we're being forced to live the same day over and over again. Ask Gilgamesh when he gets back. He's been looking into it."

"How does he know its name?" I asked.

"He spelled it out on his Ouija board. Eih Cra is everywhere in this building." He glanced around. "I can feel him. It gives me the chills." Billy crossed his arms and shivered.

This was a little mind-boggling. There was a presence in the hotel? Billy's wooden teeth began to chatter. "Is there anything we can do for you?" I asked.

"G-G-Get me a blanket."

I took one from the floor and tucked it around his legs. "Turn on the radio," he said. "I think *The Shadow* is on."

The radio was a big mahogany box with two dials. I spun one, and a deep voice boomed, "Who knows what evil lurks in the hearts of men? The Shadow knows!"

I felt a chill at the sound of the announcer. Cindy crossed her arms. I wished we had time to hear the whole program. But, like The Shadow himself, we had a mystery to solve. "We're going to go now, Billy. It was nice to meet you."

"Good luck to you," the dummy said. "And goodbye to your sidekick."

# CHAPTER TEN

# CHECKERED PAST

I closed the door, the sound of the radio program echoing in the room.

"We just spent the last ten minutes talking to a ventriloquist's dummy," Cindy said. "Do you find that a little...oh...odd?"

"Odd?" I said. "We *are* in Saskatoon, remember. Maybe things were even weirder in the past. I'm more worried about this presence he kept talking about. I can't put the pieces together."

"Maybe we should just find the kid," she said. "He must be the key."

"You're right, I bet." I crossed the hall and knocked on room 649. No answer. I knocked again and turned the knob. The door creaked open.

We saw a boy wearing the same little suit as the ghost. Except he wasn't shimmering. I couldn't see through him. His cheeks were pale, but with a pink tinge and dirty stains, as though he had just been crying. He was wearing shoes.

"This isn't the ghost," I whispered. "This is the real Archie."

"Great green sunfish!" Cindy exclaimed.

"H-hello," he said. "Wh-oo are you?" Archie looked from Cindy to me. "Are you here to play? Did Mom and Dad send you? Have you seen them?"

"I'm Walter, and this is Cindy," I said. "We come from far away."

"A different time zone completely," Cindy added. He stared at her as if she were speaking pig Latin. "We're friends."

"Friends?" he said slowly, his voice cracking, as though the word was hard to say. He swallowed. "I like friends. I don't have any right now. I did once, but they're gone. They didn't like me. So you're my new friends? I-I like games, do you? Checkers. Cards. I like books, too. My favourite is *The Wonderful Wizard of Oz*."

"Well, you sure came to the right hotel," I said.

He scrunched up his face into a look of confusion. He unscrunched his face. "You'll play with me," he whispered. I wasn't sure if it was a question or a command.

"Please. Please. I'm sad. So sad."

"Uh, sure," I said.

He went over to the bed and began setting up the checkerboard, humming to himself.

"Isn't he supposed to be in the hospital?" Cindy asked quietly.

"Yes," I answered so only she could hear. "It was late on the 14th – today, that is – when he passed away. Unless the newspaper report was wrong."

"He does look pretty healthy, for a dead boy," Cindy said.

"I'm ready!" he shouted. "You'll play with me."

"Will you take the first round?" I asked. "I have to make a call."

Cindy nodded and went over to the bed, saying, "I have to warn you, Archie; I'm the queen of checkers."

"You'll lose," he said. "And I'll be happy."

I went to the corner of the room, standing next to an antique desk that, well, wasn't antique, since I was in the past. I flipped open the trans-dimensional, time-travel-proof cellphone and dialed my home number. The receiver crackled and buzzed, for about half a minute.

"You win," I heard Cindy say in the background. "That was fast."

My phone found a line. Mom picked it up on the fourth ring. "Hello, Margaret Bronson speaking."

"Hi, Mom," I said. "I'm calling from the past. I have a couple of questions."

"You haven't talked to any strangers, have you?"

"Does a ventriloquist's dummy count?" I explained everything quickly. "So I need to know who this Eih Cra is. Can you check your ghost databases for the name?"

"I will. I should have the synchrotron results on that ectoplasm later this evening, too. Now don't be out too late."

"I'm in the past, Mom. I'll arrive home the same time I left."

"Oh, right! I can't keep track of all those time travel rules."

Something suddenly occurred to me. "Will you check one more thing? Will you find out why there weren't any stairs up to the sixth floor of the Bessborough? I find it a little odd. Just phone Miss Schaefer, the librarian in the Local History Room."

"Okay, I'll get back to you as soon as possible."

I hung up, slipped the phone into my pocket, and Velcroed it shut.

"You win again!" Cindy sounded surprised. "I've never been beaten so quickly! This kid is amazing."

"I'm a good winner," Archie said. He turned his big, determined eyes to me. "You'll play now, and you'll lose too."

I shook my head. "Not right now. We're here to talk to you, Archie. Where are your parents?"

He cringed and hung his head. "They – they went away. They'll come back someday. I think. It's been a long time."

"Where did they go?" I asked.

"Far, far away, but they'll come back. They said so. That's why I'm here. I'm waiting for them."

"How long have you been waiting?" Cindy asked.

He stared at her. Blinked. A lost look came over his face, and tears formed in his eyes. "I...I don't know. I can't count that high. I miss them."

"It's okay." I put my hand on his shoulder; he was cold as a marble statue. I still found it eerie that he was solid. According to the newspaper, he should be breathing his last breath about now. Instead, he was here – and alive. The report must have been wrong. I decided to write a letter to *The StarPhoenix* complaining about bad reporting. Then it dawned on me that the reporter would have gone to that great news office in the sky by now.

Archie shivered. "You will read to me," he said, sniffling. "You'll read to me, and I'll feel better. Mommy and Daddy always read to me. It's almost my bedtime. Every night they read a chapter from my book before I go to sleep. So you will have to read it."

"We only have time for a paragraph," Cindy said, "then you'll have to answer more questions for us." She hunted around for a book. There was a small suitcase on the floor and a deck of cards on the desk beside an old-style black phone with an oversized handset. Nothing else. "You don't have a book."

"We'll take the elevator," Archie said. "There are books in the library."

He jumped up and went to the door. He opened it and peered into the hall as though he was afraid of something. Did he know about Eih Cra too? Or even sense the presence? He stepped out into the hall.

"Wait," I said. "Wait for us!" But he was already halfway down the hall.

We followed. "He beat me at checkers," Cindy said.

"Oh, don't get sour."

"You don't understand. No one has ever beaten me three times in a row. It's like he's a checker genius."

Archie was getting even farther away. For a little kid he could really motor. "We should have brought a leash," I said.

Archie looked to his left down the other hallway and let out a sudden screech that made all the hairs on the back of my neck sprout. He paused for a moment, sucked in a deep breath, and screamed again. This time the lights above us rattled.

"What's up with him?" I asked, breaking into a run.

"IIII-VVVE got you!" an angry voice cried. "Now I've got you!"

CHAPTER ELEVEN

# I'LL TAKE DOOR NUMBER TWO

A black shape charged around the corner, robes flapping like giant crow's wings, long arms stretched out – Gilgamesh. His eyes were gigantic and glowing like lamps, as though he were battery-charged. In his hand, with sparks flying from its top, was a magic wand.

Archie leapt out of the way like a frightened jackrabbit and darted down the hall.

"Stop, you rotten little Munchkin!" Gilgamesh swung the wand, and an electrical charge burned a hole in the rug just in front of Archie, making him jump backwards. "You're going to tell me everything! Every single thing!" Gilgamesh lunged, his arms stretched to their full length. He grabbed onto Archie's suit coat.

Archie looked over his shoulder, his eyes wide with absolute brain-numbing fear. He was turning as pale as ivory. Gilgamesh lifted the wand. Archie suddenly yelled – a frightened, high-pitched shriek that vibrated with all his pain and fear, growing louder and higher so that it seemed to make the very walls of the hotel shake. Both Cindy and I put our hands to our ears.

Even Gilgamesh halted, momentarily looking frightened himself. He grimaced and lifted his wand, the top of it crackling with energy. "Stop! Stop! I said stop!"

"You stop!" I shouted, banging headlong into Gilgamesh from behind with my best impression of a football tackle. He yelled, bonged his head against the brass fire extinguisher on the wall, and crumpled to the floor, his robes fluttering around him. He lay still, his purple Swami hat unravelling like a snake on the floor.

"You knocked him out," Cindy whispered. "At least I hope you did."

The three of us stared, frozen like ice carvings. I breathed in a few seconds later. "We can't be that lucky," I said, stepping around him. Gilgamesh's creepy eyes stayed closed. Cindy leaned down, squinting in the darkness.

"Don't get so close," I warned.

"He's out cold," she answered. "He won't be getting

up for a long –"

His hands, like two crab claws, snapped out at her.

Cindy jumped back, landing in a fighting stance, her arms up and ready to deliver quick punches. Gilgamesh rose to his feet; he seemed even taller than before. "You will give the boy to me," he said.

Cindy and I stood between him and Archie. "What's the big idea of picking on a little boy?" Cindy shouted. "What kind of magician are you?"

She stepped slowly back, Archie cowering behind her. She pressed the elevator button.

"You stupid monkeys!" Gilgamesh hissed. His eyes had grown even larger, glowing like 100-watt bulbs. "He summoned you, didn't he? Are you demons? Are you servants of Eih Cra?"

"No!" I said. "We're detectives!"

This confused him. "I just want the boy." Slobber dripped from his bottom lip; his long hair hung limply, soaked in sweat. "Only for a minute. I won't hurt a hair on his head." He took a step towards us. The wand was glowing. It most likely wasn't real magic, but it might be electrical. "Release him! You cannot protect him from me. I am Gilgamesh the Great!"

I had read and reread the manual on *Negotiating With Crazy People* (it comes in handy when dealing with my parents, or teachers). The manual said that the best thing to do was to keep him talking. "Why do you want him? What's he done to you?"

"What's he done?" Gilgamesh grunted. "Everything! That's what he's done! Everything! All of this!"

The elevator made a *DING* and the door opened. Archie jumped on.

Gilgamesh pulled back his arm to unleash the power of his wand.

"Back off," I said. "Or I'll..."

I couldn't think of a threat.

"We'll kick your butt," Cindy finished. "Tae kwon do you to dust. You'll wish you'd never met us."

"Oh, it is you who will wish we'd never met," he said. He narrowed his eyes. "You'll end up like the other two. No one has seen them for ages. The monkey got them."

He must have been talking about Janet McGaffin and John Williams. Or else there was someone else who had disappeared here. But why was he babbling about a monkey? Either way, it was a good time to make our escape. I quickly turned to jump into the elevator.

The doors had already closed. Archie was gone.

At the same time the doors to the second elevator opened. I grabbed Cindy's hand and yanked her through the opening. We had escaped!

Unfortunately, the elevator was missing.

We fell into deep darkness.

# CHAPTER TWELVE

# FALLING, FALLING, FALLING...

Most people believe you scream when you fall. I actually was too busy hyperventilating to scream. Cindy, on the other hand, seemed to still have full control of her lungs.

"AHHHHHHHHHHHHHHH!" she screamed. Then she gulped air. "AAAAAAAAAHHHHHHHHHH!" she continued.

Between bouts of hyperventilating, some oxygen seemed to rise slowly into my brain, and a plan suddenly formed in my mind. I un-Velcroed my pocket and pulled out the cellphone. Of course, I didn't have time to make a call, but I had remembered that it could create a time field around whoever was holding it – a protective barrier. Which meant one of us didn't have to fall to the bottom of the elevator shaft and be turned into a flapjack.

I slipped the phone into Cindy's hand and pressed 9-1-1. Blue ribbons of energy shot out of the receiver, wrapping her up like a glowing Christmas present. She looked at me with wide-eyed shock. "What are you –"

She froze in mid-air.

I continued to fall, Cindy glowing above me like a star in the sky.

"AHHHHHHHH!" I yelled. "AHHHHHHHH-HHHHHHH!"

And down I plummeted, my stomach feeling like it was hurtling up my esophagus. I thought of all the things I'd left undone in my life. I hadn't found a sasquatch or grown a moustache. Nor had I figured out the ghost train of St. Louis. That's St. Louis, Saskatchewan, by the way. And now I was going to meet my doom at the bottom of an elevator shaft. I felt bad for all the tricks I'd played on the principal and for calling Cindy a sidekick. My poor parents would be devastated. Mom would blame it on the vampires, of course, and Dad would curse the aliens of Alpha Centauri.

I thought about all the math homework I wouldn't have to do. I wouldn't have to finish that essay for Principal Pytlowany, either.

Then I thought...I'm doing a lot of thinking. Time had either slowed down or my synapses were working so fast it seemed like time had stopped.

"AHHHH," I continued to scream. "UHHHH... hmmm," I said finally, scratching my chin. There had to be a bottom somewhere. I looked down, but it was only deeper darkness.

I crossed my arms. "Hmmmph," I said. "Apparently there isn't a bottom."

Suddenly: KERSPLASH!

Apparently I was wrong.

My momentum carried me deeper into the liquid, and I had the sensation that I was floating in goo. Like a cork with a brain, I shot up into the air, sucking in the mightiest breath of my life. I sucked in two more, nearly as mighty, filling my lungs.

I dog-paddled towards the side, and found that the stuff I was in was wet all right, but it wasn't water – it stuck to me like liquid honey. It smelled vaguely like rotten fruit.

"Okay," I said to myself. "You're alive. That's good. You're in a pool of unidentifiable goo. That's bad."

I reached the side and felt around the wooden walls of the elevator shaft. Eventually my fingers stumbled across a ladder. My first real piece of luck in the last little while. I pulled myself upwards; the gumbo seemed to be holding on as though it didn't want me to leave. With a SHA-PLOP, I popped out, glad I hadn't lost a shoe.

The goo made my hands slippery, so I held on with all my strength and continued climbing. There wasn't any light above me, not even a glowing Cindy.

I climbed higher and higher, until I started to sweat. A humming sound reverberated through the shaft. The elevator was running. I panicked for a second, wondering if I was about to be crushed, but it dawned on me that the sound was too high above me.

Finally, a light appeared. The ladder ended at a square opening.

It was the basement of the Bessborough. I'd obviously fallen quite far down in order to climb up to the basement. I stepped out under a bare light bulb. All around me were the massive foundations of the hotel, pillars of concrete that held the whole structure up. There were also several piles of coal.

I examined my hands. The goo had dried and looked, unfortunately, like green snot. Ectoplasm. Ghost goo. But why was there so much of it at the bottom of the elevator shaft?

I rubbed it off my hands and my face, wishing I could take a shower or be sprayed clean by a firehose. I hunted around for stairs.

The question was, how long would Cindy hang in the middle of the air. Would she fall? What floor was she on?

I dashed from room to room, ducking under giant pipes. One room had boilers big enough for the Titanic, clanging out the heat. Another chamber was stuffed with broken chairs. I stumbled across the lost-and-found area: hats, purses, dolls, canes, and rows of wooden legs.

Who would forget their wooden leg? I wondered. Or was it a service of the hotel to provide wooden legs to their customers? Maybe there were lots of one-legged people in the thirties.

I was still pondering this when I discovered a set of stairs and climbed them two at a time. Finally I reached what must have been a main floor. There were carts of food and a service elevator. I paused before the elevator, then decided I couldn't risk riding in another one.

I passed a mirror, apparently there for the staff to check themselves before going out in public. I looked as though I'd landed in a pool of Brylcreem – my hair was slicked back and hard. Several strands of ectoplasm dangled from my nostrils looking like – well, you can guess. So I wiped my nose and found the next set of stairs.

The door opened onto the ground floor. In my time it was where the check-in desk was located, but here in the past it was a diner. Several citizens were sitting there eating. The men had hat hair – their fedoras hung from hooks behind the booths. The women were in fancy dresses and stylish hats that tilted to one side and had many-coloured feathers. The smell of frying steaks and food hung in the air. I wondered who owned the fedora hat store in Saskatoon. He must be a millionaire by now.

I glanced out the front doors, to see Saskatoon of the 1930s. It was dark, but an old-style car – a Studebaker – putted by. The buildings were all shorter, and the Midtown mall had disappeared – at the end of the street was the train station. It was snowing again, the heavy flakes swirling around the street lights. Another Studebaker went by, the same style. It must have been a popular car back then. As popular as fedoras. Maybe they had a two-for-one deal.

A third Studebaker putted by. It was odd that there weren't any other cars. I didn't have time to figure out what was going on, though.

I ran up the stairs to the mezzanine, zipping past the check-in desk and whipping by the library. I stopped suddenly and backed up.

Archie was sitting inside the library on an ornate couch, reading *The Wonderful Wizard of Oz*.

# CHAPTER THIRTEEN

# SUDDEN APPEARANCES

"**W**hat are you doing here?" I asked.

"I'm reading," he said, without looking up. "Where is Kansas? And what does this big word mean: C-Y-C-L-O-N-E?"

"Well, we definitely aren't in Kansas. And I don't have time to answer your questions."

"You'll read to me," he said. "Won't you? It's past my bedtime. Someone should be reading to me."

"Not now! Did you see Cindy? What about Gilgamesh?" I glanced around. There was another boy in the library, reading a newspaper – all I could see were his legs and his tiny hands holding both edges of the paper. He shook one hand in the air as if it had fallen asleep. I glanced past him, at the desk clerk. He quickly looked away, as though he'd been staring – he was obviously the suspicious type, but I suppose that was part of his job. He wrote something on a piece of paper, and slipped it into a metal cylinder. He turned around to the pneumatic tubes. I heard the hiss of a vacuum, then he shoved it in and it shot upwards. Before there was e-mail, there were pneumatic tubes.

"Gilgamesh doesn't matter now," Archie said. "You'll read to me and I'll feel better, won't I? That's what matters."

"Hey Archie, buddy, I can't read to you now. I have to find Cindy."

"But...but...I want you to." And, just like that, he began to cry, giant tears streaming down his face, his pale cheeks getting all splotchy. He looked like a human Niagara Falls.

"Okay, okay," I said. "I'll make a deal with you. First, we'll find Cindy, then I'll read to you. Any book you want."

He sniffled, dug a hankie out of his pocket, wiped his tears, and blew his nose, making a honking sound that any Canada goose would be proud of. "Yes," he said, "it's a deal. But I only read about Oz."

"I kinda figured that out." I grabbed his hand; it was ice cold. We took about two steps; then I froze – I had missed a clue. Man's best friend is a dog, but a detective's best friend is his intuition. And my intuition was ignited, rattling like a piston in an airplane engine. I had missed several signs right under my nose.

I let go of Archie's ice-cube hand, crossed the floor, and tore the paper away from the little boy.

Billy, the talking dummy, looked up at me, a wicked grin on his wooden face. "Hello," he said, "having a nice day?"

"Billy! Are you spying on us?" I asked.

"I'm Buster, not Billy! I'm the best dummy ever!" I noticed that this dummy had no chip out of his cheek. It was Billy's replacement. "And I wasn't spying! I was catching up on the news. Did you hear about the family that went out for a drive in their Studebaker? They crashed through the ice. Poor Ma and Pa. Dead and gone, never to be seen again."

Archie's eyes grew wide. "Nnnno," he whispered, "that's not true."

"You know it's true, Archie. Blub, blub blub, down goes the car. Under the ice. There's the Tortles, sleeping with the freezing fishes."

"No," Archie said, covering his ears. He made a blubbering sob and began to wail, a long cry of sadness. His wail rose louder than a siren.

Buster laughed, a wooden rattle-like sound. "Toughen up, kid."

"Don't pick on him!" I shouted.

"You're in way over your head, bub. You have no idea where you are. Or how things work here. This isn't a normal day. You have no idea what you're dealing with."

"Listen, Munchkin, I'm catching on quick." My intuition fired. "You! You made a signal to the front-desk man," I said. "You waved your hand a few minutes ago, and the desk clerk sent a message in the pneumatic tube."

"I did no such thing."

"He signalled Gilgamesh, didn't he?" I asked, pointing at the desk man, who was nervously shuffling papers.

"Perhaps I'm just down here taking a break." Buddy crossed his legs. "The magic life is tiring, you know. Entertaining all those crowds. Pretending to be a dummy."

I took three giant steps back and grabbed Archie's hand. He was moaning now, oversized tears dripping down his face. "C'mon," I said. "It'll be all right. We'll find Cindy, we'll read to you, and we'll get you someplace safe and warm. Okay?"

Archie nodded, mopping his cheeks with his sleeve. "I'll be a big boy," he said.

"Good! Good boy. We better get going."

I ran toward the elevator. Somehow there had to be a way to get to Cindy. I'd have to find ropes, or break the

"Break in Case of Fire" glass, yank out the firehose, and feed it down the elevator shaft. It would take some serious climbing to get down to her, but I had practised enough at Vic's Vertical Walls to do it. It was a good plan. I ran it through my head once more to double-check it. I went over it a third time, looking for weaknesses. Just as I finished, the door to the elevator opened, and Cindy stepped out.

"Hey, Wart," she said. "Your mom called; she wants you to call back."

"Hey...but...how did you get here?"

"Well," she said, looking calm as could be. The elevator doors closed behind her. "That force field you put me in didn't completely freeze me. I just floated there. After awhile I discovered that I could move by kicking my feet slowly. I gradually worked my way to the wall, grabbed the ladder, turned off the force field, climbed up to the nearest floor, and pried open the door with my flashlight. Then I got back on the elevator, and here I am." She paused. "Thank you, by the way; it looks like you saved me from a fate worse than death – spelunking in slime. Nice greasy hair!"

"Hey! That's no way to talk to me! You should have more respect. I'm the CEO of our company and I –"

The elevator doors clunked open again like a sideways mouth, spewing out a cloud of thick, dark smoke.

"Get back!" a shadow yelled inside the smog. "Get away from me!" The elevator shook as someone or something was thrown against the wall. "I know you! I know you! You're Eih Cra!"

A sound that I never want to hear again thundered in my eardrums – deep all-powerful laughter that was half roar. There was a flash, bright as the sun. Two figures were briefly outlined in the light, one gigantic and looming.

Gilgamesh took one tottering step into the lobby, his hair smoking.

"AAACH!" he cried. He put his hand to his head. "That hurt." He collapsed.

# CHAPTER FOURTEEN

# THE BOGEYMAN

"Run! Run! Run!" Archie yelled. "It's the Monkey Monster! The nightmare creature!" His voice was so shrill my eyes watered. I grabbed his hand, Cindy snatched up his other one, and we ran, pulling him between us.

I glanced over my shoulder. Buster was poking Gilgamesh, trying to wake him. The dummy looked up. A black, clawed foot stepped out of the elevator. It was attached to a gargantuan leg. Something, a winged creature, was squeezing itself out of the elevator. Two ebony hands reached toward the dummy.

I didn't see what happened next. We were too far down the hall.

"Into the men's bathroom," I yelled.

"I can't go in *there*," Cindy said, pulling Archie the other way towards the women's washroom.

"Well, I can't go in there!" I said. We ended up barrelling straight ahead, bashing French doors open and stumbling into one of the large ballrooms. The ceiling was high above us. The tables were set with white linen, plates and silver cutlery glittering.

Cindy found a chair and propped it against the door. "That'll hold him for about a microsecond," I said.

"I'm doing my best," Cindy yelled.

"There must be a way out." Already the creature was slouching down the hallway, each step shaking the floor. We ran to the back of the ballroom. "What is that thing?" I asked. "Ghosts I can handle, but is it some transdimensional ogre?"

"I got a good look at it," Cindy said between breaths. She shuddered. "It looked kind of familiar."

"It's the Monkey Monster," Archie said. He kept glancing over his shoulder; he'd suddenly developed a nervous tic. "It's – it's from my nightmares. It scares me every night. It's terrible and evil, and it took my parents away. It took away John and Janet too."

"Who?" I asked.

"My friends. They came to visit me. Followed me here, just like you did. And the monkey took them. Hid them away in a trunk."

Suddenly a revelation hit me with the force of a battering ram. "John Wilson and Janet McGaffin!" I exclaimed. "Is that who you mean?"

Archie nodded. "Yes, those were their names."

"They were the ones who travelled back in time in the sixties," I said to Cindy.

"I remember," she said. "I do pay attention to some of the things you say. What happened to them?"

"They were bad," Archie said. "So the monster took them. They deserved it. They didn't want to play."

The kid was a confused mess. And frankly, my brain didn't work all that well when I was in full panic mode. We came to the exit door at the other end of the ballroom, just as the French doors behind us were smashed open. The creature, still cloaked partly in smoky fog, looked left and right. With its wings spread, it was gigantic.

Cindy stared at it.

"Let's go," I said, tugging on her arm.

"But it's so familiar," she said. The monster flapped its wings and let out a screeching cry. "Uh, we better not stick around for a closer look." It shot into the air, arcing towards us like a missile. Its wings clipped the chandelier in the centre of the ceiling, and the light crashed to the floor, taking out three tables.

I yanked open the door, shoved the two of them in

front of me and slammed the door behind us, just as the monster's head hit it. The door cracked. I tumbled down the stairs behind them, hoping the hallway was too small for the thing to squeeze down.

We were in another lost-and-found room, cluttered with broken toys and boxes of wooden legs.

"Why all the legs?" Cindy asked.

"They seem to collect them," I said as we looked for a door. We ran from wall to wall.

"This room goes nowhere," Cindy yelled, sounding panicky. "We're trapped!"

"Not yet," I said. I dialed the TD2 phone.

"Hello," my mom answered.

"Hi, Mom! I have an –"

"Walter!" Mom interrupted. "I analyzed that ectoplasm. It's the most powerful ecto substance I've ever seen. Can you bring back more of it?" She was so excited she didn't give me a chance to answer. "Oh, I don't have any records of Eih Cra. Are you sure he exists? Is the spelling right? And I phoned that librarian about the stairs at the Bess. There were always stairs there. You must have been lost."

Stairs? What was she talking about? Oh, I'd asked her to find out about them, too. "Look, I can't chit-chat, right now, Mom – there's a creature chasing us. It's big and has wings, and it looks like a monkey." I was trying to sound calm, but I was afraid my voice would crack at any second. "It's like King Kong on steroids. I think it's Eih Cra. I'm wondering if Dad could come by and help. Maybe bring his stun gun or the neurozapper."

"Your dad's at a Conspiracy Theory meeting," she said. "Can you call back?"

"Mom! We're in trouble. This thing'll be down the stairs any second now."

"I'm sure it *seems* like an emergency, but every time you call it's an emergency. How am I supposed to know whether this is a real one or not? And did you – *bbxzzzt-crackle.*"

"What? Mom, your voice is fading."

"*bzztcrackl* – clean your room, promise – *zzzt.*"

"Clean my room? What? Get down here."

"*zzzt* – how do I get – *zzzt* – there?"

"You just press the buttons on the elevator. On the mezzanine floor. First press the fourth-floor button, then the –"

CLICK. All the lights on the phone went dark. Archie had reached out and touched it. "What is that?" he asked. "Who are you talking to? Your mom? Will she visit too?"

I jammed the power button, but there was no sign of life. I shook the phone. Maybe if I switched the batteries around, it would start up again.

SCCREEATCH! The creature was coming down the stairs, wings or claws scratching along the wall.

CHAPTER FIFTEEN

# EIH CRA REVEALED!

Cindy grabbed a wooden leg. Archie cowered behind us. "He's coming," he whispered. "He's coming to get you." I grabbed another leg and gawked quickly around. There was a laundry chute across from us, but before I could point it out, the creature shoved its way into the room, stopping between us and the chute. How had it squeezed down the stairs?

"You will be my friends," Archie said. "Swear you'll be my friends."

"We are," I said, pushing him behind me. Cindy waved the leg back and forth. The monster lumbered into the dim light, its face a mass of shadows. A good detective can always come up with a plan in an emergency. I thought a moment, then turned to Cindy.

"Any plans?" I asked. "Just want to see how you react under pressure."

She shook her head. "I don't think brute force will work. Music may soothe the beast." She whistled the theme from *Star Wars*. The monster roared, fangs gleaming in the darkness. "Maybe not."

"You will be my friends," Archie said again. For some reason, he didn't sound scared. "You'll read to me and play with me. And you'll tell me that you love me."

"What?" I said.

He was serious. "It's my monster," he said, as though he were talking to a child. "If you don't do what I tell you, it will take you back to its nest and stuff you in a trunk. Later it will eat you. That's what happened to John and Janet."

"What are you talking about?" I asked.

"You will stay here. You two. And grow up and be my parents, and it will all be happy ever after. We'll be home. We'll finally be home." He suddenly pushed under my arm so that he stood right in front of the monster.

"Archie!"

"It's my monster," he explained again. He snapped his fingers, and the monster stepped into the light. Slaver dripped from dark, twisted lips. It blinked eyes as big as baseballs, glowing red. But its nose was a human nose. It somehow had Archie's face.

"It looks a bit like Archie," I whispered. "Except really, really ugly."

"That's why it was so familiar," Cindy said.

Nothing was making sense. My brain had thudded to a stop. I looked at the leg Cindy was holding and at the leg in my hands. There wouldn't be that many wooden legs in one hotel. Hundreds of one-legged people would have had to visit and forget their legs. That was impossible, especially since the Bessborough had just opened. I thought of the maids, how they had looked the same, the male guests, each with their fedoras. The Studebakers. Only *The Wonderful Wizard of Oz* in the library. The lack of stairs.

"You're Eih Cra," I said. I wasn't talking to the monster, but to the boy.

"Archie," Cindy whispered. "Eih Cra is Archie spelled backwards."

"I'm Archie," he said. "You know that. I'm Archie."

"Explain this," Cindy said.

My detective's brain was humming along like a Mercedes. "We're not in the past," I answered. "We're not even in the real world. We're in a world Archie created. That's why there are all these wooden legs. Archie must have been down to the lost-and-found room and all he remembered was seeing a wooden leg. That's something that would really catch a little kid's attention." I thought of something else. "The numbers on the rooms are jumbled up because he can't count that high."

"What could have caused all this?" Cindy asked.

"It's like this: every once in a long, long while a ghost feels so much pain and grief that it can actually form a new world, a space where it last remembers being happy. That's where we are right now."

"You two will be my friends forever," Archie said. "You'll grow up and get married and be my parents."

"I'm not marrying him!" Cindy shouted.

"That's for sure!" I added. "Her fish jokes would drive me batty!"

"You will be my mom and dad," he repeated.

"Your parents are dead, Archie," I said, slowly. "You're not even a real boy any more. You're just a ghost. You can be free of this place. Of all the pain you're feeling. You don't need us to be your parents."

"Don't say that!" he yelled, and the beast behind him roared, shaking the room. The wooden legs rattled in the boxes behind us as though they were trying to run out of the room themselves. He covered his ears. "If you say that again, my monster will eat you."

"Leaping longnose sucker! That's why it looks like a monkey," Cindy said. "There were flying monkeys in *The Wonderful Wizard of Oz.* So," She took a step forward, "it isn't real. And all we have to do is face it in the real world and it will disappear." She took another step and swung the wooden leg, striking the Monkey Monster between the ears.

It shook its head. It didn't disappear. Instead, with lightning-quick reflexes, it grabbed the wooden leg and snapped it in two.

"Or not," she said.

I reached into my pocket and blinded it with the flashlight. The beast reared back, and in that second I yelled, "Go!"

Cindy read my mind. She launched ahead of us down the laundry chute. Before the door closed, I dropped my wooden leg, grabbed Archie, and pushed him into the chute. I followed him down, rattling and rolling into the darkness.

# CHAPTER SIXTEEN

# GOO-ED TIME

We landed in a pool of ectoplasmic goo, sank deep down, and popped up like sputtering rubber ducks. "Not again!" I said.

"My hair," Cindy yelled. "It'll never be the same!"

For a moment I couldn't find Archie, but then I heard splashing. I dragged him to the side of the pool. Kicking and screaming, he flailed the whole time, but he didn't pull me down. We climbed out onto a dirt floor. The dirt stuck to the goo, turning into something close to mud.

"The ectoplasm is a by-product of Archie's mind," I said. "I've never seen so much in one place."

"So he created everything. When? How?"

Archie was coughing up his own ectoplasm. I patted him on the back.

"When he died. Maybe even that exact moment this whole place sprang into being."

"You keep talking about me as if I'm dead," Archie said. "But I'm here. I'm right here. I'm not a ghost."

"No, Archie," I said. "There was an accident. Do you remember going on a drive with your parents? The car fell through the ice. Do you remember that?"

"No," he said. "They left me forever. The Wicked Witch took them, that's what happened. She came out of the sky on her broom and laughed and took them away. You'll replace them."

"We can't do that," I said. "We want to go home. We're just kids ourselves. We have parents too."

The chute above us shook; then creaked, the tin suddenly expanding as the Monkey Monster somehow forced his way down. Boards snapped in two, and bricks rained into the ectoplasm. "You will love me," Archie said, his voice hoarse. "You will."

We dragged him through the underground of the Bessborough. The halls went this way and that. Several came to dead ends with rooms full of giant furnaces; another was filled with stacks of wooden chairs. Finally we found the elevator. I pressed the button and we waited. The creature roared behind us, as though being separated from Archie was making it even angrier. It rounded a concrete pillar.

The instant the elevator dinged, the monkey charged. We jumped in, and I jabbed the button. The doors closed just in time. "Up! Up! Up!" I urged.

"We *are* going up," Cindy said. "That's what happens when you press the UP button."

The elevator shot higher, rattling as we stood there clutching Archie between us. A loud bang came from below us. "It sounds like he broke down the doors," Cindy said.

The elevator lurched, and the cable motor above us began to growl and complain, as though it were carrying too much weight. "He must be climbing the cables!" I said.

The doors to the eighth floor opened, and we shot out of the shaking elevator.

"I have an idea," I said.

"It's about time," Cindy said. "You *are* the CEO, after all."

If I'd had enough time, I would have thought up a comeback, but I was too busy running, dragging Archie along. We dashed down the hall and climbed a set of stairs that led to a thick door with a sign saying: HOTEL PATRONS NOT ALLOWED BEYOND THIS POINT.

"Is this your plan? I have the feeling we're going to be cornered up here."

"Just keep going!"

I dragged Archie through the door.

"Where are we going?" Cindy asked.

"Up," I said. "To the very top of the Bessborough."

"We can't go up there," Archie said. "It's the highest room. It's the monster's den. There are bones there. And skeletons. And bad things. Terrible, bad things."

We passed the tops of the elevators, where the whirring cables pulled the elevators up and down. We dodged between sparking electrical boxes.

An iron ladder led upwards to a trap door.

"I don't go in his den," Archie said. "Not his den. That's where the nightmares come from."

"Are you sure we should go up?" Cindy said. "I have a bad feeling about this."

"I'm supposed to get the bad feelings," I said, as a joke. "I'm the worrywart, remember? If I weren't, things might turn out really bad. I'm just trusting my instinct. I've got to be right."

I climbed, pulling Archie along, Cindy pushing him from the bottom. He was growing lighter as we climbed. "Noooooo," he whispered. "Not up there. That's where everything horrible sleeps."

I pushed on the trap door, and it didn't budge. But hair stuck to my fingers. Monkey hair. I set my legs, shouldered the trap door open, and climbed in. Archie fell to his knees the moment I pulled him inside.

We were in the tower on top of the Bessborough. From outside, it looked majestic. But inside the square, high-ceilinged room was dingy and dark, with two yellowed windows letting in moonlight. There was a trunk in the corner, several half-eaten dinners, and a pile of rotting banana peels. It smelled like an overripe garbage pit. And in the centre was the monkey's nest. "No, we can't be here," Archie said. "We can't."

I wasn't sure what we'd find. I knew there had to be something to solve our situation. When, on impulse, I dragged Archie to the nest, he whimpered and moaned.

"No," he said. "I don't want to look in there. I can't look."

"Are you afraid of the monkey?" I asked.

"No. I'm afraid of the words. Of the papers. And the pictures. Don't make me look."

The nest was littered with white paper – hundreds and hundreds of copies of *The Saskatoon StarPhoenix*, all with headlines: PARENTS DIE IN ICY MISHAP! BOY NEAR DEATH IN HOSPITAL! Crumpled pages with photos of the Studebaker in the ice were everywhere, scattered beside pictures of Archie in the hospital.

I reached down and picked up a paper. Archie hit my arm, trying to knock it out of my hand. "Don't look! It's bad! Bad words!"

I held tight, picked up another paper. They were all from the day after the accident. "Can you read this?" I asked. He looked so lost, but I had to be hard on him, mean even. The monkey was screeching, bounding its way up the ladder. "Quick! Can you read this?"

"P-a-r-e-n-t-s," he said. "Parents."

"Read faster, please," Cindy said.

"D-i-e. Parents die." He held his head with both hands and swallowed a sob. I pushed the paper closer to him. "B-o-y. Boy near death." He pointed at the picture. "Is that me?" he asked. "I think that's me."

The monkey squeezed through the trap door. Its wings unfolded as it turned towards us, eyes burning with anger. It opened its mouth, revealing long fangs. It took a step towards us. And another.

Cindy and I grabbed Archie and backed up, until we hit the wall. I searched left and right, but there were only two windows, and we'd have to go through the monster to get to them.

Archie was clutching the paper, his hands shaking as he stared at the picture of himself. "That's me," he whispered. "Me."

The monster came closer, so close that I could count its sharp teeth. It smelled rotten. It looked from Cindy to me, trying to decide which one to eat first. The creature slowly reached out a giant clawed hand, so big it could crush my skull with one squeeze.

"That's me," Archie said, his voice a moan. "That's my parents in the car. They died. They died." He paused and swallowed as though he were swallowing a stone. "I died. I – I shouldn't be here. None of us should be here."

The monkey stopped reaching, and looked down at Archie. The creature appeared shocked. "You shouldn't be here," Archie said. "Goodbye."

The monster sniffed once and shook its head. It opened its mouth as if to argue with Archie. Suddenly it began to grow smaller and smaller until it was the same size as us. It quickly shrank and disappeared with a soft *pop*.

I let out my breath.

"Just in time," Cindy said.

I wiped sweat from my forehead. "Yep, I don't like to cut it that close. You're a good boy, Archie."

We both looked at him, surprised to see that he was fading too. "Goodbye," he said. He was see-through now, his feet bare. "Thank you." His permanent frown slowly became a smile. Then something like a grin. "I'm happy." His voice warbled slightly. "I'm going to see my parents now. I'm going home. Thanks, you two. You're good friends."

He faded completely away.

Cindy and I stared at the spot where he had stood.

"He's gone," she said. "He's going where he'll be happy."

"Yeah, I won't ever forget the look in his eyes when he suddenly became happy again." I put my hand on Cindy's shoulder. "You did a good job."

"We both did."

The hotel began to shake around us as though an earthquake had struck. We struggled to keep our feet. The shaking stopped.

"I think we better be going now," I said. "Something awful is about to happen."

"Let's get moving!" Cindy added.

We had taken two steps when a voice said, "Let us out! Let us out!"

CHAPTER SEVENTEEN

# THE FORGOTTEN ONES

"What?" I asked.

"Who?" Cindy said.

We stopped by the trunk. It was locked. I hunted around until I found a heavy brick. It took four good hard swings before the lock busted off. Two kids popped out, like a jack-and-jill-in-the-box, about the same age as us. They were dressed in old-style clothing, maybe from the sixties.

"Who are you?" I asked.

"John," said the boy. He had wide shoulders and looked more determined than scared.

"I'm Janet," the girl answered, glancing warily around the room. She had her hair done in pigtails.

"Of course," I said. "I've met you already, Janet."

"I – I don't think so. I don't know you."

"Uh, in the future, I mean. I *will* meet you."

"Pardon?" she said. "I'm not sure what you mean."

"It's a little complicated," Cindy added. "How did you two get here?"

"We followed Archie," Janet explained. "We were at school decorating the gym for Fun Week, and he appeared and led us here. We thought he was a lost little boy. He wanted us to play with him. Then his monkey put us here."

"How long have you been in the trunk?"

"Only a few hours," John said.

"But it felt longer," Janet added.

"It's... Uh..." I didn't want to shock them too much. "It may have been a lot longer. This is 2004."

Their eyes widened as they did the math. "We've been here for over forty years."

"Not necessarily," Cindy said. "Time is different in this ghost hotel."

"That's right," I said, already putting together a theory. "In fact, I'd say time is frozen here. It's the same two days again and again. Archie was reliving the day of his parent's death and the day of his own death. Maybe he was trying to understand it all. But he couldn't, until now."

"That must be it," Cindy continued. "The same two days over and over. But little or no time has passed in the real world. Maybe only a few minutes have passed for you two. When you get back to your own time, that is."

"This isn't the real world?" Janet said. "What is it then?"

"Yeah, where are we?" John demanded.

The Bessborough groaned and shook on its foundations. With Archie gone, I suddenly realized there was nothing to hold the building together.

"We don't have time to explain," I said. "One thing I know for sure is that we don't want to be trapped here forever. Follow us!"

As we ran, bricks and beams began falling all around us. We slid down the ladder like firemen, and scrambled past the sparking elevator motors. The four of us stopped at the elevator.

There was a crowd waiting there. Gilgamesh was cradling both of his dummies in his hands. The desk clerk stood beside him. "You defeated Eih Cra," said Gilgamesh.

"Yeah, I guess," Cindy said.

"It was really Archie," I added. "He created this ghost hotel. He created you."

"What!" Billy, the dummy, pinched his arm. "I feel real. I do." He punched Buster in the arm.

"Ow!"

"He feels real too," Billy said.

Gilgamesh pulled on his beard, obviously thinking deeply. When he spoke his voice was sombre. "Now everything about this place – and about me – makes sense. I've never felt completely real, completely whole. We were always living the same two days over and over again. The boy just dreamed us up. We were only props in his world. So somewhere out there is a real world where there once was a real Gilgamesh the Great. Archie must have met him in the hotel. I was just created from the boy's memory."

"That's right," Cindy said. "You're like a photograph. You're just a copy, not the real thing. He was a very powerful ghost."

"But I still don't understand one thing," Gilgamesh continued. "Why are all of us still here? Shouldn't we be disappearing?"

"Until the boy's world implodes around us, you'll exist," I explained.

"But where do we go next?" Gilgamesh asked. "Are we like rabbits pulled out of a hat? Do we change into doves?"

"I don't know," I admitted. "But I don't want to be caught here when this ghost version of the Bessborough implodes. I think you have one chance. All of you. Get on the elevator and punch a few numbers, whatever comes into your head. And when the doors open, get off there. Maybe you'll be home. Maybe. Or in whatever dimension you belong."

"Thank you," Gilgamesh said. "Perhaps we'll meet again."

"Uh, I hope not," I said. "No offence, but I want to stay in my own dimension for awhile."

"Good luck," Cindy said to all of them.

"Thanks for getting us out of the trunk." John shook my hand. Janet smiled.

"I'm pretty sure you'll make it," I said to the two of them.

Cindy and I stepped on the open elevator. She punched the fourth-floor button, then the fifth and sixth buttons at once. The elevator groaned and shot downwards so quickly that I thought my feet would go through my brains.

The elevator began to shrink until we were forced to crouch over; just as suddenly it expanded to ten times its size and we were like tiny gerbils on the floor.

With a SNAP it came back to its normal size. The doors rumbled open.

We stepped out. A woman with a poodle stood and stared at us; apparently the sight of two ectoplasmed detectives had surprised her. Her husband, talking on a cellphone, stopped talking, his mouth hanging open. Everyone stared at us, our hair slick with goo.

"Howdy folks," I said. "I hope you enjoy your stay more than we did."

"I need a bath," Cindy said.

Mom was at the desk, gesturing dramatically and waving her cellphone like a light sabre. She must have sped straight down here after I called. "I have to go back in time," she yelled. "Do you know the code? My son and his sidekick are there. I have to rescue them. It's your fault if he's caught in some other dimension."

"Hi, Mom!"

She turned. "Forget everything I just said. Walt! You're all right." She ran over and hugged me to her chest, the familiar scent of garlic filling my nostrils. I was home. She patted my head. "And you brought some more of that ectoplasm home. How clever! The car's just outside."

The doorman opened the door for us.

"You two look like you've been through the wringer." He paused. He looked us up and down. "You know," he said, "I have this feeling that you did a really good thing."

"We were just doing our job," I said. We stepped out into a freezing, normal November in Saskatoon.

CHAPTER EIGHTEEN

# OZ WELL THAT ENDS WELL

The next day I marched into Victoria School, showered and clean, not a sign of goo anywhere. It had taken four cotton swabs and fifteen tissues to clean my ears and nose. I had slept like a log in the middle of a quiet forest. I was proud and pleased with how I, with a little help from my sidekick Cindy, had solved the mystery.

I had to stop calling her a sidekick, I reminded myself. She deserved better.

"We did it," I said to Cindy. She too had showered and was wearing her black *Look Out Behind You* sweatshirt. "Another notch on our belts."

"Yep, it felt good. We rocked, so to speak."

"You worked hard, Cindy. I officially declare you a –"

"Master detective? Senior investigator? Official officer."

"No," I said. "You really did a great job. We're a great team. Therefore, I'm making you the co-CEO of the agency."

"Wow! Cool! When do I get my name on the card?" she asked. "And my own TD2 telephone?"

I paused. "Soon, very soon. I do want to say, as a charter member of the Walter Biggar Bronson Ghost Detective and Time Travel Agency, that you were simply marvellous and that the future of our company will –"

A hand clapped down on my shoulder. "Mr. Bronson, good morning."

Principal Pytlowany looked down at me. He held out his hand.

I gave him five.

He looked at me with absolute and utter confusion. I shook his hand.

"Mr. Bronson, you appear to have forgotten that your paper is due."

"My paper!" I put my hand to my forehead. "But I was busy saving the universe. Well, not our universe exactly; it was an alternate universe inside the Bessborough. There was this boy named Archie, though some people called him Eih Cra – you see, that's Archie backwards, and he was a ghost and –"

"I'm only interested in seeing that paper, Mr. Bronson. I'll give you an extension until first thing tomorrow morning."

"Tomorrow!" I let out my breath. "I should be able to do it."

"You *will* do it. And since you have such a wonderful imagination, along with the paper, I'll expect a five-page short story."

"What!" I said.

Cindy laughed.

"Did I say five pages? I meant ten. You choose the topic." He paused. "Actually, I'll choose the topic. Write a story about a wild gopher emergency."

Busted! I hung my head. "I will, sir."

He walked away, his job done.

"As my partner," I said, "it will be your job to help me with the paper."

"Fat chance, Wart," Cindy said. "I'm too busy to help. As co-CEO of the Walter and Cindy Ghost Detective and Time Travel Agency, I have a lot of extra work to do."

"Walter and Cindy Agency? You can't just change the name."

"I just did. I'm co-CEO, remember? We need letterhead and cards too. How does pink grab you? Something with flowers on the side."

"What! Not pink! No!"

"You won't have time to help me select colours. You have tons of homework to do, remember?" She smiled. "But I know how you can go home and get started right away."

"How?"

"Just click your shoes together and *poof* you'll go home. It worked for Dorothy in *The Wonderful Wizard of Oz*."

I clicked my shoes together. "There's no place like home. There's no place like home."

I was stuck in the hall. I stopped clicking my shoes together because people had started to stare at me. Might as well face it, I had a lot of writing to do. Where was a cyclone when you really needed one?

ACKNOWLEDGEMENTS

Thanks to Andrew Turnbull, the Delta Bessborough, Robert Currie, and the Nutana Community Association Recreational Badminton League.

# ABOUT THE AUTHOR

Arthur Slade is one of Canada's best-known and most respected writers of fiction for young readers. His novel *Dust*, set in Depression-era Saskatchewan, won the Governor General's Award for Children's Literature, the Mr. Christie Book Award, and the Saskatchewan Book Award for Children's Literature; it was also nominated for a prestigious American award, the Edgar, for mystery writing.

His other books include *Tribes*, *Draugr*, *The Loki Wolf*, and *The Haunting of Drang Island*.

In 2002, Coteau Books launched Art's exciting and entertaining new series, *Canadian Chills*. The first title, *Return of the Grudstone Ghosts*, won the Diamond Willow Award of the Saskatchewan Young Readers Choice Awards in 2004.

Arthur Slade was raised on a ranch in Saskatchewan's Cypress Hills and now lives in Saskatoon.